A King Production

MAFIA
Princess

Stay Rich Or Die Trying

PART 4

A NOVEL

JOY DEJA KING
AND CHRIS BOOKER

This novel is a work of fiction. Any references to real people, events, establishments, or locales are intended only to give the fiction a sense of reality and authenticity. Other names, characters, and incidents occurring in the work are either the product of the author's imagination or are used fictitiously, as those fictionalized events and incidents that involve real persons. Any character that happens to share the name of a person who is an acquaintance of the author, past or present, is purely coincidental and is in no way intended to be an actual account involving that person.

ISBN 13: 978-0986004513
ISBN 10: 0986004510
Cover concept by Joy Deja King
Cover layout and graphic design by www.MarionDesigns.com
Typesetting: Keith Saunders

Library of Congress Cataloging-in-Publication Data;
A King Production
Mafia Princess Part 4 by: Joy Deja King/Chris Booker
For complete Library of Congress Copyright info visit;
www.joydejaking.com
Twitter @joydejaking

A KING PRODUCTION

A King Production
P.O. Box 912, Collierville, TN 38027

A King Production and the above portrayal log are trademarks of
A King Production LLC

Dedication

This Book is Dedicated To My:
Family, Readers and Supporters.
I LOVE you guys so much. Please believe that!!

—Joy Deja King

A KING PRODUCTION

MAFIA
Princess

PART 4

Stay Rich Or Die Trying

A NOVEL

JOY DEJA KING
AND CHRIS BOOKER

Prologue

Looking through the large, tinted Gucci frames, Semaj looked down from the second level of the small warehouse as her men packed kilos of cocaine into several large storage bins. 200 of those kilos were due to be delivered to Sosa back in New York by tomorrow, so everything needed to be packed and shipped correctly. The slightest bit of confusion could tip off the authorities, leaving Semaj to have to chalk up a loss to the game, something she wasn't used to.

"This is the last shipment for the week," Vikingo said, walking up beside Semaj with a clipboard in his hand. "I was thinking that maybe we can take the rest of the day off and go to my mother's house for dinner," he suggested, leaning in and kissing her on the cheek.

Semaj didn't even get a chance to respond to him when a loud commotion erupted outside of the warehouse, immediately getting both her and Vikingo's attention. Seconds later, two or three of her field workers ran into the warehouse stumbling and falling into the storage bins.

"The poachers! The poachers are taking everything!" one of the workers yelled out through his short breath.

"Shit! Not again!" Vikingo responded, taking off down the steps.

Semaj took off too, breaking the heels of her designer shoes in the process of running down the steps. By the time she made it to the entrance of the warehouse, Vikingo had already jumped into his golf cart and was heading in the direction the workers came from.

"How many of them were there?" Semaj asked one of the workers as she walked over and helped her off the ground.

"Four ... maybe five of them, Senorita. They all had very big machetes and had masks over their faces," the worker informed her.

Vikingo looked out into the piece of land that was stripped to the soil where coca plants once were. The poachers had gotten away by the time he got there. A whole acre was missing this time, a lot more than what the poachers normally took. It was common in almost every cartel to have poacher problems. They pretty much stole anything that wasn't tied down, but in this case the coca plants were their targets.

"Daaaaaaaaammmmnn!" Semaj yelled out, pulling up and jumping off her golf cart. "They went from five to ten plants to..."

She couldn't even let out the surprising number of plants missing as she looked out into the field. "You gonna let these poachers take everything I got?" Semaj joked, playfully tapping Vikingo on his ass.

Vikingo didn't feel like playing around. He was mad as hell and didn't think that it was a laughing matter at all. For someone to be brave enough to steal from a cartel was a serious matter, especially a cartel as big as the Espreilla Family.

"Don't worry about it. We'll catch 'em," Semaj assured, wrapping her arms around his waist from behind.

Semaj cut the joking out seeing how much it was bothering Vikingo and became a little more serious herself. She did not think that poaching was that big of a deal, considering the fact that she had more acres than she could count, but as Vikingo looked out into the patch of dirt, he could sense that something crazy was going to come about behind this. He felt disaster striking and the only thing he wanted to do was get in front of it before it hit home, because one thing he knew about Colombia and the drug game was that nobody was promised to live to see the next day. It was a dog-eat-dog world, and in order to stay alive, violence had to be the first thing you reverted to. Anything other than that and you'd end up being the next meal of the day. That was the last thing he wanted to be, and if Semaj didn't smarten up quick, that was exactly what she was going to turn into -- the meal of the day.

"We need more guns," Vikingo said, in a frustrated tone before walking off back to his cart.

Semaj felt a sense of unspoken fear behind Vikingo's request. As she walked back to her golf cart she whipped out her phone and punched in a couple of numbers before pulling off. She was going to make it her business to get Vikingo everything that he needed no matter how much it was going to cost. She was quickly becoming focused, and that was her best bet if she knew any better.

Chapter 1

Over the past year, Colombia had officially become Semaj's home. It was amazing how she had matured in such a short span, studying the culture and taking some time out to learn how to read, write, speak, and understand the Spanish language. She really didn't have any other choice in the matter, because walking in her grandmother's shoes required her to step up her game to full capacity.

The drug game was still the family business and cocaine was at a high demand in the States. The production of cocaine wasn't the problem; it was getting it over to the United States. Transporting it by submarines wasn't flying in the United States. They had the Atlantic and the Gulf of Mexico on lockdown, so it was going to take longer and cost more using different routes to get it in. That was the only headache Semaj was having -- that, and a problem with poachers.

"Make sure it's deep enough. I don't wanna have to smell his body when I drive through here," Semaj said as she walked over and took a seat under a tree to get out of the blazing sun.

Vikingo was up to his chest in dirt from digging a ditch. His whole shirt was drenched in sweat and the mosquitos didn't mind taking a few bites out of him.

"You know, I could have paid somebody to do this," Vikingo said, jumping out of the ditch.

"Now what fun would that be? It seems like this is the only time I get to spend with you," Semaj joked, coming from under the tree and passing him cold water.

"I hope it don't be like this when we get married," she said, leaning in to kiss him.

He wrapped his arms around her waist and was about to enjoy a few more kisses until Semaj playfully broke away. "Come on, let's get this over with," she said, walking over to the dead body lying a few feet away from the ditch.

She began nudging the body with her foot in an attempt to roll it over into the ditch. The poacher was too big for that, and instead of helping Semaj, Vikingo laughed while trying to encourage her to use a little more force.

"He stole 200 plants in less than an hour," Vikingo teased. "200 plants is a lot of money, Mama," he joked.

200 plants *was* a lot of money, and that wasn't a laughing matter in Semaj's eyes. Instead of nudging it, she began kicking the body until she jammed her big toe.

"Shit!" she yelled, jumping up and down on one foot.

Vikingo thought it was hilarious watching Semaj

hold her toe. She looked mad, but at the same time she looked like she was holding back a smile. Vikingo walked over to the body, put his foot on top of it and kicked it into the ditch. He then walked over to Semaj, reached down, scooped her off the ground and sat her under the tree.

"I'ma kick ya ass for laughing at me," she said, tossing some cold water onto his back before he walked away.

Although they laughed and joked around, they both knew how serious poaching was and how much money was lost behind it. Poachers stole just about anything of value that was in open fields: Coffee, corn, wheat, and in this case, coca plants. There was only one way farmers dealt with poachers in Columbia, and that was to kill them, if they ever got caught on their land. The same rules applied with Semaj; that's why Vikingo was standing in the baking sun burying one.

One would think that after you killed one or two, other poachers wouldn't try their hand, but it was the total opposite. This was the eighth poacher Vikingo had buried in the past month, and it seemed like the grave sites around the coca fields weren't enough to deter the poachers. One thing was for sure and two things were certain: Vikingo had plenty of bullets and plenty of time on his hands to catch up on his target practice.

A little boy ran through the Water House Village dipping in

and out of the heavy traffic of people in the marketplace. Water House was a village inside of Kingston, Jamaica that was known for, and thrived off of violence. This was where Ox grew up as a child before moving to Cherry Gardens, where he started to make money in the drug game. A lot of people didn't know it, but Ox had a pretty nice-sized family, including three sisters and one brother, and that didn't include all the aunts, uncles, and cousins on both his mother's and his father's side of the family.

During the many wars on the streets and the multiple flu epidemics Jamaica sustained, most of Ox's family was killed off, and those that were still alive were scattered about in Jamaica and in the United States.

"For you," the little boy said, slamming a brown folder onto the table when he walked into the small leather shop.

Paulette looked up from the sewing machine to see the little boy still standing there waiting for some kind of compensation for the errand. Paulette looked at him and smiled. She picked up the envelope and took a peek inside. Seeing that the contents were what she wanted, she reached into her pocket and pulled out a wad of money. The little boy's eyes got wide at the sight of all of that American money. When she peeled off a few bills and passed them to him, he darted out the door like a racehorse.

"Is that it?" Paulette's boyfriend Patrick said, coming out from the back.

"Yeah mon," she said, tossing him the envelope.

He pulled everything out and spread it across the table to get a better look. There were surveillance pictures of Sosa sitting in a coffee shop, pictures of Sosa dropping off and picking up Nyala from school, and a copy of Nyala's school records, along with the pictures of Sosa's 2013 BMW 760. The private investigator Paulette had hired had done his job, which was harder than most jobs he'd taken. Sosa was a difficult woman to catch up with, especially since she made a conscientious decision to stay under the radar. She did her business in the streets, but most of the time it was done using somebody else's name and face instead of hers.

"You sure dis 'er?" Patrick asked, looking at the picture of Sosa sitting in the coffee shop.

"Me know it's 'er. I neva forget a face," Paulette answered, pushing the pictures to the side, then returned her focus to her sewing.

Paulette only had to look at Sosa's picture one time to remember how Ox used to keep Sosa close to him. She used to tease Ox all of the time, telling him that Sosa was going to end up killing him when she found out he was fucking half of the women in Jamaica. Paulette was right about that, because Sosa was the last person Ox saw before a bullet entered his skull. Just the thought of her brother's death made Paulette's blood boil, so much that she couldn't focus on doing anything else but gutting Sosa like a fish.

"Pack a bag. We leave tomorrow," Paulette told Patrick before getting up from the sewing machine.

She felt like she didn't want to delay the process any longer than she had to. The quicker Sosa was dead, the better; but one thing Paulette had underestimated about Sosa was her will to live and the extent she'd go to just to stay alive.

Semaj walked over to her computer, turned it on and waited for her phone to ring. At least twice a week she would Skype with her Dad, being that she didn't have time to travel to London to see him. It was a good way for them to stay in contact and see each other's physical wellbeing. It took a few minutes but Semaj's father, Mitch, was pretty much on point with his phone call. Semaj clicked on her screen and there he was with a huge smile on his face.

"Hey Princess," Mitch said, seeing Semaj take a seat in the chair.

"Hey Daddy. What's going on over there?" Semaj said, noticing people walking back and forth behind him.

"Oh, I am just doing a little...cleaning," he stuttered. Semaj smiled. She of all people knew when her Dad was either telling a lie or trying to hide something from her.

"Daaaad, don't lie to me," she said, scrunching up her face at him.

Mitch had to laugh to himself knowing he couldn't hide too much of anything from her. He sat there for a second scratching his head, not really wanting to tell her right away that he was moving back to New York.

"Come on Dad, why would you wanna move back there?" Semaj asked, after he broke down and told her.

London was cool but it was only a certain amount of time before Mitch got homesick. They loved him in London and he was in total control of the drug market, but his heart was, and always would be, Brooklyn-bound. The few visits that he'd taken to New York over the past year were more than a tease, especially since he had the kind of money that turned the City into one big playground.

"Look Princess, I am not gonna move back to New York permanently, just an extended stay for about a month or so. Right now I'm a little homesick, you know," Mitch stated.

She looked into the computer screen and at the sad look her Dad had on his face. Semaj couldn't argue with him about that. There were times when she got a little homesick too. Just hearing about all of the fun that Mitch had while he was visiting the city made Semaj start thinking about all the fun she used to have ripping and running around Brooklyn.

"So did you think about where you want to get married?" Mitch asked, trying to change the subject. Semaj chuckled and put her head down, knowing Mitch was going to get a kick out of the location. It was a known fact that once you've lived in New York you become attached to the city, and with Semaj, she was no different than anybody else.

"New York, Daddy," Semaj giggled. "New York."

Paulette couldn't take her eyes off the picture of Nyala to save her life. The little girl looked just like her mother who had passed away several years ago. It also made her think about Nyala's father, Ox, who was Paulette's baby brother. Nyala was the last of the females left in their family and Paulette wanted her back. In fact, she needed her back to ensure the family's blood would go on for generations to come. A female is the only one who can guarantee that, and being as though Paulette was too old to have any more kids and her sisters had died before they could give birth to a girl, Ox's daughter was the last hope. Paulette was in a position to do just about anything to get Nyala back and raise her as her own, even if that meant killing Sosa and anybody else that stood in her way.

Chapter 2

The cool night breeze brushed up against Semaj's face as she drove the golf cart towards the location Vikingo directed her to over the walkie-talkie. When she finally made it to the edge of the water bank where the coco field ended, Vikingo and several other men had gathered around two bullet-riddled bodies lying on the ground. Immediately, Semaj noticed a large section of coca plants missing from the field. She really couldn't see the full extent of the damage because of the night, but in all actuality, there were three times as many coca plants missing, and if given enough time, the poachers could have cleared a few acres.

"How much this time?" Semaj asked, walking up to Vikingo and looking down at the bodies.

"We won't know until the sun comes up. A couple of them got away," Vikingo said, holding a large assault rifle in his hand.

Poachers had been a problem for Semaj in her coca field for the past few months. They would come in the middle of the night, snatch as many plants out of the ground as they could and vanish into the darkness. Each plant with its roots still attached to it could be sold on the streets of Colombia for pennies. The more plants, the more money, and in some parts of Colombia poverty was high. Some poachers actually lived off poaching.

"What happened over there?" Semaj asked, seeing an additional small group of men standing around another body.

"Oh, that's Manu," Vikingo said, putting his head down.

Manu used to be a field worker until Semaj bumped him up to security. He was the hardest worker Semaj had and for many reasons she had a great deal of respect for him. She kicked the hell out of one of the poachers' dead bodies as she walked over to Manu's body. He had taken a bullet to his chest in an attempt to stop them.

"Now they're becoming violent," Semaj said, kneeling down next to Manu.

She was a little concerned now, being as though this was the first time one of her people had been killed by a poacher. Usually they would just come and snatch as many plants as they could and make a break for it.

"Don't worry. We'll tighten up the security around the perimeter," Vikingo assured her.

"I need you to shoot and kill every poacher that steps foot in this field, and I want their bodies buried right here," Semaj said, pointing to the patch of dirt where the plants were taken from.

Semaj was more than irritated; she was starting to

feel like she was being tested. If word got out that people could steal from the Espreilla Family, Semaj would be looked upon as being weak. Weakness wasn't an option for a Drug Lord in Colombia. Other Drug Lords would eat her alive and she knew it.

"Come in!" Sosa yelled, after hearing a knock at her door. She didn't have to pick her head up from her computer to know that it was Penny, her good friend, walking though the door.

"The truck just pulled into the docks," Penny told Sosa as she took a seat on the edge of the desk.

Sosa looked up at Penny and then closed her laptop. The shipment came a day late this month, something that was unusual. When Semaj said something was going to be delivered on a certain day and at a certain time, it was going to be done to the letter. Sosa reached in her desk drawer and grabbed a .50 caliber Desert Eagle and a large yellow envelope before heading out of the office. Penny was right behind her pulling her hair back into a ponytail and readjusting the .45 Millennium from the back to the front of her waist.

"You know, that guy Qua still wants to talk to you," Penny said, walking behind Sosa as they made their way down the hallway to the docking area.

Sosa wasn't trying to hear a thing about Qua right now. Her focus was on what was going on at the dock. She cautiously walked up to the back door and took a peep out the window before she opened the door, seeing if the regular guys were delivering the shipment or if it was somebody different.

"What time were they supposed to be here?" Sosa asked Penny with a curious look on her face.

Sosa was still in the drug game on a heavy scale and often used her business as a drop-off spot for large shipments of cocaine coming from Colombia. She had the second largest coffee shop in New York, complete with a second floor that had a kitchen and a bar. Pretty much anybody that was somebody would eat and drink there, so its popularity provided a blanket for her illegal activities going on in the back.

"They are definitely a day late," Penny said, looking down at her phone.

Sosa put the envelope on a shelf and then proceeded out the door onto the small dock. The driver and his crew were already unloading box after box onto the platform.

"Hey! Hey!" Sosa yelled, getting Javier's attention.

He stopped, but the rest of the workers continued unloading.

"You're a day late. Why are you a day late?" Sosa asked, holding the large gun down by her side.

"Look, I only do what I am told. I don't ask any questions," he responded, wiping the sweat from his forehead. "I deliver, I get paid, and that's it."

"Alright! Alright!" Sosa said, waving him off with her gun.

She immediately pulled out her cell phone dialing

Semaj's number. It rang a few times and went to the voicemail. It wasn't like Semaj not to call Sosa if there was a change in the delivery, but since Semaj wasn't answering her phone, Sosa had to make the decision to either keep the cargo or send it back with Javier until Semaj confirmed the late delivery.

"Look, take all of this shit back where you got it from. I don't know what's in these boxes," Sosa snapped.

"What are you talking about?" Javier said, with an attitude. "You know..."

"I am not asking you, I am telling you," Sosa said, with a straight face as she tapped the side of her leg with her gun.

It had to be done like this. No amount of money in Sosa's eyes was worth going to jail for, and being as though this was a day-late drop, Sosa wasn't going to take any chances, especially since she couldn't get Semaj on the phone to confirm. Rules and regulations were put in place specifically for situations like this; one of the more serious of them was that if a delivery was early or came later than the time that it was supposed to get there, you don't accept it under any circumstances. Javier looked at Sosa and then at her gun. As bad as he didn't want to, he had to load everything back onto the truck. Sosa didn't even stick around to watch. She went right back into the coffee shop and locked the door behind her and Penny.

"So what are you going to do?" Ron asked Qua, turning

the music down in the car.

It wasn't just in New York; the lack of cocaine was eating the whole East Coast alive. Border Patrol was cracking down on everything that was moving, and the Coast Guard and the Navy were working overtime in the Gulf of Mexico. That meant it was going to be harder to get cocaine into Mexico, which would in turn pour out into the States. When drugs can't get into the States, drug dealers call it a "drought." It could be weeks before some coke would manage to surface, and when it did, the prices on it would be so high a nigga would hesitate to buy it.

"I know somebody with some work," Qua said, thinking about Sosa.

"We should be straight in a couple of days. We gotta stretch the little bit of coke we got left," he explained to Ron as he looked out his window.

It was unfortunate, but the drought had reached Qua as well. Even his connect, who was a major player in the game, had run out and was on standby. This was the first time in years Qua had gotten caught up in the drought and it bothered him that the only person he knew for sure that had some product was Sosa, his only competition in the city.

Times like this made him wish he was still connected with the 16 Tent. One of the many benefits of being a member was that you never had to worry about running out of cocaine. Now, Qua was in a predicament where he had to swallow his pride, tuck his tail in between his ass and purchase cocaine from Sosa. It was either that or just wait for his connect to get right. Qua really couldn't afford that. He would lose clientele and money, and more than likely it would make it into Sosa's hands eventually, which was something else he wanted to avoid.

"Why didn't she take it?" Agent Davis asked Javier when he got out of the truck.

"I don't know. She complained about me being late. She probably figured it out," Javier responded, wiping the sweat from his forehead.

Getting large amounts of cocaine into America was a task by itself, but distributing it out to the States was when the risk factors kicked in. Over 90% of cocaine came from Colombia. It traveled from Colombia to the Caribbean Islands and then into Mexico. From Mexico, it came into the United States, more than likely through manmade tunnels that stretched into Texas. For it to get to the East Coast, Atlanta was the distribution state. Highway I-95 was used to get cocaine up and down the East Coast to cities like Columbia, South Carolina, Charlotte, North Carolina, Richmond, Virginia, Philadelphia, and New York.

Sometimes I-95 could be a sure prison sentence because highway patrol, DEA agents, ATF, and the FBI knew the highway's significance in the drug trading business. Javier just so happened to be on the right highway but at the wrong time when he got pulled over by a K-9 unit while riding through Virginia. Instead of locking Javier and his crew up, the DEA made him a deal on site. They had to know where 200 kilos of raw cocaine were going, and the person who it was being delivered to.

"I think he's lying to us," Agent Davis said to Agent King as he pulled him to the side.

"I don't know. He went straight to the location that he described to us back in Virginia. I think whoever this coke belongs to will inquire about it once they see the drugs never made it to their destination," Agent King said.

"It had to come from somewhere, and I think we should try to focus on that as well," Agent Davis responded before walking back over to Javier who was leaning up against the truck looking scared to death.

Chapter 3

Semaj stood in the shower letting the water spray over the top of her hair. Her wedding was less than three months away and the only person she could think about was Qua. It wasn't that she didn't love Vikingo, because she did, but in the back of Semaj's mind she always felt like she never truly closed the door to her and Qua's relationship before she opened another door with Vikingo. Semaj had it bad. The love that she had for Qua was crazy. So crazy that sometimes she questioned herself on whether or not marrying Vikingo was the right thing to do.

The last thing she wanted to do was hurt him. Vikingo was good to Semaj. He waited on her hand and foot, and there wasn't anything that he wouldn't do for her.

"Damn Semaj, you trippin," she said, turning the water off, and stopped talking to herself out loud.

She hurried up, got out of the shower and almost busted her ass trying to get to the toilet so she could pee. It felt like her bladder wasn't strong enough to hold it. She sat there and tried to pee but there wasn't anything coming out. Then she felt it release, but something was funny because she only heard drips hitting the toilet instead of a stream. She went to look into the toilet and saw that the water was a little red.

"What da...," she said, reaching for the toilet paper.

When she went to wipe herself she couldn't believe how much blood was on the tissue. It scared her to the point where she stood up and looked into the toilet. Thick, dark, globs of blood sat at the toilet's bottom, and more blood continued to drip down her leg. It was at that point Semaj knew what happened. She had only heard rumors of that happening when she was young but never did she think she would experience having a miscarriage.

She had only found out a couple weeks ago that she was pregnant and hadn't even told Vikingo that he was going to be a dad. She'd planned on waiting until their wedding day to surprise him with the good news. Until then, it was just going to be her little secret. Semaj stood there for a minute looking at all of the blood in the toilet and all of the blood running down her leg. A million and one thoughts ran through her mind as to whether or not this was a sign that she wasn't supposed to have any kids by Vikingo. It made her a little confused because she was just thinking about Qua right before it happened. Semaj leaned over, took one last look at her little secret and flushed it down the toilet. She walked back over to the shower and got in, but this time it was to try and wash away her depression.

It was closing time at the coffee shop, but right before Penny went to lock the door, in walked Qua and his boy Ron. Penny was shocked that he was standing there after she specifically told him that Sosa was going to call him when she got ready. One thing Penny didn't know about Qua was that he wasn't going to keep being put on hold for anybody. Most of the time if he wanted to see somebody in the city it would happen when he wanted it to. It was only out of respect for Semaj that he let Sosa get money in New York anyway. Other than that, Sosa would have been up in a cemetery somewhere pushing up flowers.

"Where Sos?" Qua asked with an attitude.

He was tired of playing the run-around games. "Like I said before. She's going to call you when she feels like talking to you," Penny shot back, now having an attitude herself.

Penny wasn't the one to be played with either. She might have had a cute baby face and spoke softly at times, but her murder game was on 100%. That's one of the few reasons why Sosa had her around.

Qua just stood there like he wasn't going anywhere until Sosa appeared. He didn't say another word and neither did Penny. When Qua tried to walk past her, Penny pulled a .45 off her waist so swiftly and smoothly that Qua didn't even have a chance to react. Ron, on the other hand, was on point, pulling his 9mm Parabellum from off his waist. Neither one of them pointed the guns at each other, but kept them by their sides as a warning.

"Ease up P," Sosa said, looking down on the whole situation from the second floor.

Qua didn't even know that she'd been standing up there the whole time. It was a good thing Sosa did say something because Penny was just about at her breaking point.

"Come on up Qua...alone," Sosa instructed.

Penny stepped to the side to let Qua go past, but kept an eye on Ron, who was smiling at her.

"She got a little fire with her Bro. Ya'll two should get married," Qua joked, walking past Penny to go upstairs.

By the time Qua got up the steps Sosa was already sitting in one of the booths waiting for him. "All this tension for an old friend," Qua said, taking a seat across from her.

"Well you know how it is Qua. Shit can get ugly in New York," Sosa responded, shrugging her shoulders. "But what can I do for you anyway?" she asked in a pleasant manner.

Qua could hardly muster up the words to say what he came for. He knew Sosa was going to love the fact that he needed to buy some coke off of her. He never thought in a million years that he would have to stoop so low, but in all actuality, he really didn't have a choice. It was either that or not eat at all until his people got right.

"I need some work. I know..."

"How much do you need Qua?" Sosa said, cutting

him off. She already knew what he had come for.

Qua knew that the product that he would be getting from Sosa was going to be raw and un-cut, so he was going to aim high, and for the best price.

"I need 100 joints for 15,000 a pop."

"I'll give it to you for 13,000 a pop if you stop fuckin' wit Raul," she offered.

Qua wasn't surprised that Sosa knew who he was buying from, being as though she was still a member of the 16 Tent. However, he was surprised that she was taking clientele from another member of the 16 Tent without the consent of the rest of the members. Raul represented Cuba, and as far as he knew, Raul was still a member. Qua may not have been a part of the 16 Tent, but he definitely knew the rules.

"I'ma stick with 15,000 a pop for now," Qua answered and then got up from the booth. "So when can..."

"Tomorrow. I'll call you," she said, answering him before he completed his question.

Qua started to leave but stopped in mid-stride. Something was eating at him the whole time he sat there in front of her, and he wasn't going to leave until he knew. He turned around to look at Sosa.

"How is she?" he asked, thinking about Semaj.

Sosa smiled. She knew that he was going to ask about Semaj, eventually. The relationship between the two was very complicated, but no matter what the situation was, there was always going to be love there. One thing Qua was unaware of was that Semaj was about to get married. Sosa knew that he didn't know, but it wasn't her place to tell him. That was something Semaj had to do on her own time.

"Another three hours and we should be in the Haiti," Patrick said, coming into the room from being outside on the deck.

For Paulette, getting into the States wasn't that easy since she didn't have a passport, or any other form of I.D for that matter. She was from a time and era where identification wasn't needed in Jamaica, and she never planned on leaving there until now. So with no proper I.D., mixed with the fact that she feared airplanes more than God Himself, Paulette was forced to take the other route, which was by boat. This was also the route other illegals took to get into the States. It went from Jamaica to Haiti and from Haiti to the Bahamas and then from the Bahamas into Florida. A trip like this could take a few days, depending on how long the boat docked at each stop.

To Paulette, it didn't matter how long it was going to take her to get there. It just gave her more time to think about Nyala and her brother Ox. Jamaica wasn't the same since Ox died a year ago, and it'd been nothing but chaos because everybody wanted to step up and fill his shoes. That meant that people had to do as much killing as he did and sell more drugs then he'd sold. Chasing that dream only ended in a lot of bloodshed. Nyala was probably the only hope Jamaica had in seeing Ox again though her, and Paulette was going to do everything in her power to make that happen, no matter who she had to kill.

"You sure you don't want me to come with you?" Vikingo asked, looking out the bedroom window at the kids playing around the helicopter.

He didn't like Semaj traveling into the United States without him, considering the fact that he almost lost her a year ago. It didn't even matter to him that she wasn't going to stay for long. He really didn't want her in the States at all.

"Papi, I'm not going to be long. I got a few things to take care of for the wedding and then I will be back. Besides, somebody gotta be here to watch over the farm," Semaj said, walking up and putting her arms around his waist.

Semaj did have a lot of things to take care of in New York for the wedding, but she also had a few other plans: to kick back with family and friends, and to see Qua. He was a chapter in her life that she had to close in order to be the wife Vikingo deserved to have. With Vikingo trailing behind Semaj's every move, there wasn't any way she would be able to get that done. There were some things Vikingo wouldn't understand, and Semaj didn't want to have to put him through that.

"Papi, I...."

For a moment Semaj contemplated telling him about the miscarriage, but ultimately decided not to. She wasn't ready for that, nor did she think that he was. All they talked about was having a child, and this kind of news would only dampen the mood. She simply placed her head against his back and enjoyed the few minutes she had left, before her helicopter took her to the airport.

Chapter 4

Nikolai sat in the lobby of the International Hotel waiting for Marco Dedaj and Raul Ordonez to join her. This was an unofficial, off the record 16 Tent meeting that none of the other members were invited to. It was rare that these types of meetings took place, but when they did, it was for a reason.

"Niko, ¿Como estas?" Raul said, as he entered the lobby and extended his hand for a shake.

Seconds later, Marco entered, also greeting everyone before taking a seat. There was a little small talk, but Nikolai wanted to get straight to the business at hand. She got up and led Raul and Marco to the unoccupied ballroom where a round table was already set up.

"Raul, you have the floor," Nikolai said, nodding in his direction.

Raul looked around. He was still a little skeptical about the road he was about to go down but at this point, there really wasn't any turning back. "Look, we all know that over 85% of cocaine is made and produced in Colombia. In fact, we all buy our cocaine from the

Espreilla family," Raul said, kind of choosing his words as he went along.

"So what are you saying?" Marco cut in, wanting Raul to get to the point. "Semaj is doing a good job with the fields in Colombia."

"Yeah, but she's weak," Raul shot back. "How long do you think she's gonna last before the local Drug Lords take over her land? Once that happens, Colombia will be up for grabs to some of the most ruthless vatos South America has to offer."

Nikolai and Marco looked at each other. Both of them had a lot of money invested in Colombia, all of which was under the guardianship of Semaj. Until today, Marco didn't have the slightest idea about the threat. Nikolai had heard a few rumors of a possible takeover but figured Semaj was capable of taking care of the problem. She wasn't so sure of that right now.

"So what do you propose we do?" Nikolai asked, sitting up in her chair to hear Raul more clearly.

Raul sat back in his chair. He really had to think about what he was about to say before he said it. His words could very well have him killed before he left the island. But again, Raul had come this far; there was no turning back now.

"I think we should kill Semaj, then take over her coca fields," Raul suggested, nervously.

Nikolai and Marco couldn't believe what Raul had let come out of his mouth. One couldn't just assassinate a member of the 16 Tent without just cause or the consent of the rest of the 16 Tent members. Even considering it was like signing your own death certificate.

"Are you crazy?" Marco asked, taking his glasses off and placing them on the table. "Do you know that all of us could be killed just by having this conversation?" he snapped.

"I know what you're thinking, but her death will not fall on anybody at this table," Raul said.

Nikolai didn't say a word. She just sat back in her chair and let it all register in her head. She always thought that Semaj was a little in over her head, but she didn't know if killing her was the solution. Actually, there was something that concerned her even more, but she didn't want to discuss it at this time. Right now, she was all ears listening to Raul's thoughts.

"So tell me, what did you have in mind?" Nikolai asked, crossing her arms across her stomach.

"I know you're not considering this," Marco said, looking over at Nikolai. Nikolai gave Marco a sharp glare and then turned back to Raul.

"I need you to excuse us for a second," Nikolai told Raul, wanting to have a word with Marco in private.

Raul hesitantly excused himself, not knowing what to expect. He wasn't sure if he had gone too far by entertaining the thought of killing another 16 Tent member. Just in case, he remembered every exit point, in the event that he had to make a break for it.

"You know, this could be beneficial for all of us," Nikolai whispered to Marco as they stood off to the side.

"Beneficial?" Marco asked with a confused look on his face. "How can killing Semaj be beneficial?" he angrily asked through clenched teeth.

Raul looked on nervously as the two men went back and forth in somewhat of a heated discussion. He only wished he could hear what was being said.

"Look, sooner or later Semaj's whole damn family will be at the Tent meetings. Mitch took over London, Sosa in New York and Semaj in Colombia. What's next? You think I'm gonna let her have my seat?" Nikolai blasted. "Soon we'll all be working for her instead of working beside her."

Marco couldn't argue with what Nikolai was saying, mainly because it made sense. Semaj, Mitch, and Sosa were in key positions in the drug trade and it was only a matter of time before they elevated above the rest. Nikolai knew it and now Marco was coming around to realize the same thing.

"You know if any of this gets back..."

"Don't worry about that. I'll make sure our name stays clear of everything," Nikolai assured. "Just trust me."

Nikolai and Marco walked back over to the table and then waved for Raul to rejoin them. Once back at the table it was quiet for a moment. Everybody kind of looked at each other. "Alright Raul. Tell us what you got," Nikolai said, finally breaking the silence.

The City's skyline never looked better for Semaj. Being in New York brought back a lot of old memories. Everything from the smell of the various types of food to the tall lofty buildings reminded Semaj of how much she'd missed being home. The first stop on her agenda was Sosa's coffee shop, and when she entered all eyes were on her. It wasn't that people there knew who she was, they were more intrigued by her entry and the two large men she had standing behind her like watchdogs. The silence was what caught Sosa's attention as she sat in the back at her table reading the newspaper. She looked up and a huge smile came over her face when she saw Semaj standing up front by the register.

"Heyyyyy cousin," Sosa yelled, as she made her way to the front with her arms stretched out for a hug.

A year felt like forever to Sosa, not being able to see Semaj, and from the smile on Semaj's face and the loving embrace she gave Sosa, it was obvious that she felt the same way. Even though they spoke over the phone and sometimes Skype, nothing was like physically being able to see family.

"When did you fly in?" Sosa asked, wiping the tears of joy away from her face.

"Today girl, and I am so jetlagged. I was about to go take a nap but I had to come see my favorite cousin first," Semaj said, pulling Sosa in for another hug.

Semaj and Sosa had a lot of catching up to do about what was going on in New York, and what was happening in Colombia. But before anything else was said, Sosa got straight to a more important piece of business that needed to be discussed.

"You know that shipment came late," Sosa said, leading Semaj back to her office.

"Yeah, well what happened?" Semaj asked with a concerned look on her face.

"Return to sender," Sosa said, taking a seat at her desk.

Semaj smiled. Sosa stuck to the code no matter what and wasn't willing to break it for anything. She couldn't afford to, considering the fact that she still owned her own coca field in Colombia, under Semaj's authority. It didn't produce nearly as much cocaine as did Semaj's fields but it was definitely enough that she didn't have to look for handouts. As long as she continued to pay her workers to maintain the fields in her absence, along with the cost of production, Semaj had agreed to help her get her product into the United States free of charge. Unfortunately, some shipments didn't make it, but that came with the game and it was a small price to pay, considering all the cocaine that did make it across.

"I'ma probably get a call about that shipment any minute now," Semaj chuckled. "So do you need something right now?" Semaj asked, knowing that it wouldn't take anything but a phone call to have the product delivered by the end of the day.

"No, not really. All I gotta do is serve...Qua," Sosa said, saying his name a little low.

Sosa really didn't want to mention his name at all

around Semaj, knowing how she still felt about him. It was evident by the way Semaj's face lit up when she heard his name. No matter how long it had been or how far apart they were, Semaj's heart still yearned for him.

"Where is he?" Semaj asked, with a smile on her face. Sosa smiled and shook her head.

"How about we get dressed and go out tonight? I am more than certain Qua will be at the club tonight. It doesn't get poppin' until late, but it's a hotspot and definitely Qua's favorite. He's always there on Friday," Sosa said, resting her chin on her hand.

Semaj couldn't have agreed more. She was looking forward to seeing Qua. There was so much she wanted to talk to him about before getting married. Semaj believed they both needed and deserved to clearly understand what went wrong in their relationship and why it didn't last. But all of that would have to wait for now. There was something else Semaj was looking forward to doing, almost as much as seeing Qua again.

"Let's go shopping," Semaj grinned, jumping up out of her chair. "We need to put a beating on 5th Avenue," she winked.

"What did they say?" Salina asked when Raul got back into the car after leaving the hotel.

"Everything's a go," he answered, snatching his tie off and throwing it into the backseat. "By this time next month, Colombia will be mine."

He looked down at the picture he kept in his wallet of his brother Julio. He would never forget the day when Julio's head was delivered to his mother's house and the rest of his body was scattered throughout the city of Havana in Cuba. When Valentina killed, she did it to make a statement for anybody else who was even considering the idea of crossing her. That's what made Valentina the most feared Drug Lord in Colombia. Semaj, on the other hand, was no Valentina. In fact, Semaj didn't even scratch the surface when it came down to putting in work the way Valentina did. Raul wanted to expose her on that and he had the right motivation to help him. Even though Semaj wasn't the one who killed Julio, Raul was going to make her pay the price for it, but not before taking everything from under her feet.

Chapter 5

Paulette and Patrick stepped off the boat and finally touched down on U.S. soil in Jacksonville, Florida. For Paulette, it was her first time, but for Patrick, he had been in the States back in the day when he used to traffic marijuana down South. An important piece of information he did remember was that once you got off the boat, you had to distance yourself from it as fast as you could, because the law wasn't far behind.

Right on point and on time, Patrick's homeboy, Doc, pulled up in a navy blue Ford Explorer with tinted windows. Doc was one of the few connections Patrick still had in the States. They called him Doc because he prescribed weed for everything. If you had a headache, smoke some weed. If you caught a cold, smoke some week. If you got shot and you were 20 miles away from the hospital, then smoke some weed. That was Doc's motto.

"Yeah mon, tell me you brought me sometin' good," Doc said, getting out of the car and hugging his old friend.

He hadn't see Patrick or Paulette since the last time he was in Jamaica. "Yeah mon. Me got you some good booda. Fresh off de boat," Patrick said, putting his bags in the car.

"Me no see a beautiful face like dis in a long time," Doc said to Paulette, walking up to her and giving her a hug. When they finally got in the car, Patrick reached in one of his bags and pulled out a pound of some of the brownest, buddiest, seedless weed Doc had seen in a long time. Doc took the whole bag, put it to his nose and took a sniff.

"Haaaa! So how much of dis chronic you got mon?" Doc asked, looking at the weed.

It took a moment for it to register in Doc's head, but when it did, he looked at Patrick with a confused look on his face.

"Dis it?" Doc asked, with one eyebrow up.

"Yeah Mon. Me didn't come 'ere to move weed," Patrick said, looking out the window to avoid eye contact.

Doc looked into his rearview mirror at Paulette, who was staring right back at him. Without any words being said, Doc knew that the reason they were in the States was far more serious than moving weed. He could tell by the cold look Paulette had in her eyes that they were there to kill somebody. Doc lived in Florida now, but he was well aware of the situation that had gone on with Ox up in New York. Every Jamaican on the East Coast knew that it was only going to be a matter of time before somebody came to avenge the legend.

"I need to get to New York mon. Can you help us?" Paulette asked, extending her arm over his shoulder with a fist full of money.

Doc looked into the rearview again at Paulette, then back at the money. From what he could see, there were 50-dollar bills on the top and on the bottom of the wad.

"Yeah, I can help you," he said, grabbing the money. "But first we gotta put dis weed up at da house. Me not driving all the way to New York wit' all dis weed," Doc said, starting up the car.

"Boy, you a crazy blood clot Rasta," Doc chuckled looking over at Patrick. "You too," he laughed, looking in his rearview at Paulette.

Trying to backtrack and figure out where 200 kilos of cocaine came from was a task in itself. Once it left Colombia it went through a long list of hands before it got to the States. It was literally impossible to find out where the cocaine originated from, but the feds knew that it had to be Colombia. Javier was one of the many pawns used by the Mexican Cartel and didn't have the slightest idea where the cocaine came from before he picked it up in North Carolina.

Agent Davis wasn't going to give up on it that easily. He was determined to find out who was bringing this large a quantity of drugs into the States. If 200 kilos was moving up I-95 this easily, more than likely the main supplier was moving ten times this much on a regular basis, and that's what Davis had a problem with. Some federal agents hated murder, others hated robbery, but it was Agent Davis who hated drugs with a passion and would go to great lengths to get it off the streets. He was every drug dealer's nightmare.

"I miss you already," Vikingo admitted, as he talked to Semaj on the telephone.

"I miss you too. But I'll be home in a couple of days, Papi," Semaj said, before being interrupted by the short Chinese lady that was giving her a manicure. "Let me finish getting my nails done and I'll call you back," she said, trying to rush off the phone.

"I love you," Vikingo said, with a smile.

"I love you too," Semaj replied, before ending the call.

Vikingo sat on top of a picnic table looking at the sun sinking into the horizon. Workers passed by him knocking the dirt off their clothes from working in the fields, which marked the end of another hard day. Vikingo was tired too and wanted nothing more than a nice warm shower and a good night's rest. As soon as he stood up to head back to the compound, the sound of gunfire erupting grabbed his attention. He looked around and tried to listen for the direction the chaos was coming from. Workers were pointing toward the northeast section of the fields, prompting Vikingo to jump into the golf cart and head in that direction.

The gunfire was getting louder and louder the closer

he got, and in the far distance Vikingo could see a few of his workers scattering away from one of the processing buildings. The cart couldn't get there fast enough, and for a split-second Vikingo was just about ready to jump off the golf cart and run the rest of the way.

Pow! Pow! Pow! Boom! Boom! La, la, la, la, la!

Bullets were flying everywhere and Vikingo damn near got hit before he even got a chance to get off the cart. It was like a war zone and Vikingo drove right into the middle of it. He jumped off the cart with an AK-47 and then ran behind a forklift where one of his workers was crouched. Vikingo asked the worker what was going on.

"Poachers! Poachers!" the worker yelled, reaching around the forklift and returning fire.

"Poachers?" Vikingo repeated, as if not believing that was correct. If it was true, they were going to the extreme to steal some coca plants. Only, they weren't stealing coca plants this time, it was already processed cocaine. The process warehouse produced over 1000 kilos a day and the poachers were sitting right in the middle of it all.

"Ola!" Vikingo yelled out to his armed guards that were on the side of the warehouse trying to get a good shot off.

He whistled and waved at them, directing everybody to back off the building. Vikingo knew that the Colombian authorities were going to be there any minute, and being as though they worked for Semaj, the poachers were going to be the ones getting the bad end of the stick once they arrived. It didn't take long either. Vikingo looked up and could see several cars about 3-5 miles out approaching with flashing lights. The gunfire had subsided, but the poachers were still inside.

"You fucked up, Vatos. You fucked up real good this time," Vikingo barked to the poachers from behind the forklift.

"This is Espreilla land," Vikingo taunted, coming out from behind the lift with the AK-47 in his hand. "Now you die."

Vikingo couldn't get another word out before multiple shots began to ring out from inside of the warehouse. He turned around and tried to run back behind the forklift, but several bullets literally lifted him up off his feet when they entered his back. One exited out of his shoulder while another remained lodged into his back. His body fell to the ground, face down in the dirt. Vikingo's men began firing at the warehouse with everything they had.

One of the workers ran out, grabbed Vikingo's hand and pulled him out of harm's way. Vikingo was hit bad but was still very much alive. Blood was everywhere, and the only thing the workers could do was apply pressure to the wound until the police got there. Once the police arrived, all of Vikingo's men ceased fire. The workers yelled and pointed to the warehouse as police exited their vehicles wearing SWAT-like gear and with mini sub-machine guns clutched in their hands.

"Policia! Policia! Policia!" they yelled as they

swarmed the warehouse with their guns blazing.

Sosa and Semaj pulled up in front of the club in a burnt orange Lamborghini Murcielago. Pulling up right behind them was Semaj's security detail in an all-black Suburban. Everybody that was standing in line waiting to be admitted into the club looked over at the duo hopping out of the sports car like they were superstars. Semaj had on an all white, sleeveless silk Missoni dress, paired with leather, wood and Lucite Givenchy sandals, and in her hand was a Kotur acrylic clutch with glitter.

Sosa showed her ass, literally, wearing a custom black leopard sequin-embroidered black cat suit, and a pair of black Giuseppe Zanotti pumps. They both looked like a bag of money.

When Semaj stepped onto the pavement, she froze. She looked at the building, remembering it all too well, and the scar that it left behind. To this day, Semaj could still taste the acid that had burned her face.

"You good baby-girl. Dis my shit now," Sosa said, walking up beside her. When the city shut down the hotel after the shooting that involved the Milano Family a couple of years ago, Sosa ended up buying the building and turning it into Club Sapphire. The hotel rooms were still optional for the public. Quiet as it's kept, Sosa bought several different buildings in the city, along with countless properties throughout the boroughs.

"Club Sapphire," Semaj said, looking up at the sign.

Sosa just grabbed her by the hand and led her into the building. Semaj's security team stayed close behind but gave her space.

"Ahhhhhhhhhh hell yeah!" the DJ yelled over the mic. "A legend just walked into the building," he said, pointing at Semaj.

DJ Red Eye knew Semaj when she was a young puppy. Murda Mitch used to bring her to the clubs all the time when she was only a teen, and dared anybody to say something about it. 10 times out of 10, people minded their own business during that time.

"Ooohhhh Shit!" Semaj said, seeing Murder Mitch walking into the building.

"Aaaaahhhh hell ya'll. We got another legend in the building," DJ Red Eye announced pointing to Mitch.

"Daaaaaadddyyy," Semaj said, walking up to him and giving him a big hug.

Sosa faded off into the crowd. She still wasn't feeling Mitch, considering the fact that he knocked off a couple members of her family. There were only two reasons why Sosa didn't pursue killing Mitch. The first was on the strength of Semaj, which was the most important, and the second was because she understood the reasons why he did what he did. He was under the impression that the Milano family had killed his only child. That's more than enough to make a man go crazy.

"So where's your soon to be husband?" Mitch yelled, over the music. "He better not have my daughter out here by herself."

"He's home taking care of something, Daddy. Now don't start no mess," Semaj joked, punching him in the chest.

It was like the music had stopped completely and the whole room became silent, or at least that's how Semaj felt when through the doors walked Qua. He was on his grown man shit too, rocking a white Louis Vuitton polo shirt, some white cargo pants, and a pair of white Louboutin Rollerboy Spikes.

"Aaallll man we got another legend in the house. It's gonna be a party tonight," DJ Red Eye shouted out.

Semaj appeared star-struck the way that her eyes locked onto him. Qua looked sexy as hell. He had a fresh Caesar cut, rose-gold Cartier watch on, and from the way his shirt conformed to his sculpted body, it was as though he was still working out daily.

"You gon' say something to him?" Mitch asked, pushing her chin up to meet the rest of her mouth.

They both laughed at that for a second. Semaj had every intention of speaking to Qua, but she was taking pleasure in simply admiring how fuckin' sexy he looked, as he walked over to the VIP booths. His body language spoke a thousand words that only Semaj understood.

"I'ma go get us something to drink," Mitch said, chuckling as he walked off.

A vibrating sensation on her leg snapped Semaj out of her daze of lusting over Qua. It was her cell phone vibrating against her leg through her clutch purse. She reached in and grabbed it, only to see Vikingo's picture on the screen. For a few seconds Semaj debated on whether to answer the call or let it go to voicemail, and she quickly decided to opt for the latter. A singe of guilt shot through Semaj as she tossed the phone back in her purse, but a stronger emotion was in control. Semaj felt this was her moment to have her face-to-face with Qua, and nothing or no one would stop her.

Doctors frantically tried to stop the bleeding coming from Vikingo's back and shoulder. The AK-47 bullets ripped through his upper back, leaving two holes the size of golf balls. The exit wound was a little smaller, but was just as hard to close up. The bullet entered near the center of his back and doctors weren't sure whether or not it had done any serious damage. Maria, Semaj's younger cousin, stood off to the side watching the doctors work on Vikingo. She tried over and over again to call Semaj but she wasn't getting any answers. The only thing she could do was keep trying in the hope that Semaj would eventually pick up.

"Come on Semaj. Pick up," Maria mumbled to herself with Vikingo's phone at her ear, as she continued to watch the doctors patch him up.

"So you're gonna act like you didn't see me," Semaj said, walking up to Qua's VIP booth.

He lifted his head up from his iPhone to see Semaj

standing in front of him looking as beautiful as he'd remembered her. In regard to her comment, he honestly hadn't seen her when he walked through the door, mainly because he wasn't expecting to.

"Damn Maj, long time no see. How you been?" Qua asked, in a calm manner. He didn't want Semaj to see how excited he really was to see her.

"So you don't want to stand up and give me a hug, or are you too smooth for that?" she asked, with a smile on her face.

"Why would I wanna hug you? Ain't you about to be a married woman?" he shot back.

Semaj stood there stunned that Qua was aware she was getting married. Only a few people were in the know about her upcoming nuptials, so she was perplexed as to who would feel the need to let Qua know about it.

"What makes you think that I am getting married?" she asked, with a curious look on her face.

Qua didn't say a thing. He simply stood and gently lifted her hand up so they both could get a better look at the large rock on her finger. Semaj felt kind of stupid that she'd left the ring on, knowing that she was gonna run into him tonight.

"Qua..."

"Naw, its cool ma, me and you happened a long time ago. Sometimes in life things don't always go the way you plan," he said, gently letting her hand go.

It didn't seem like Qua was saying much, but his words cut through Semaj like a razor. She could see the hurt and disappointment in his eyes. It damn near brought her to tears. The man that she had loved for so many years was about to make a permanent exit out of her life and she wasn't ready to let that happen. Qua began to walk away and the knot in her stomach kept getting bigger and bigger with each step he took, until finally, Semaj could no longer hold back.

"Can I please have a hug?" her voice pleaded. Semaj needed to feel his arms wrapped around her, if only for one last time.

Qua continued to walk away but she reached out and grabbed his arm. It didn't matter how much of a boss Semaj was or how much work she had put in over the last couple of years, she was naturally submissive to Qua and had been since the day they met. It wasn't the fearful submission, but rather the humbling type that came from love.

Like Semaj, this time Qua was unable to deny his love. His heart wouldn't let him. He slowly pulled her towards his body and wrapped his arms around her. Semaj dropped her purse trying to hold on to his back so tightly, as if she would never have the chance to hold him in her arms again. His muscular physique devoured her petite frame. She needed this so desperately, and for that moment during their embrace, Semaj believed all was perfect in her world. She felt safe and secure, without the slightest worry. But most of all she realized their bond was still intact and the love they shared was still there.

Chapter 6

"Damn, the city hasn't changed one bit," Semaj said, looking out the passenger side window as her and Sosa passed by Marcy Projects.

"You know the hood is gonna be the hood," Sosa smiled. "What are you thinking about?" she asked Semaj, seeing a look of despair on her face.

Semaj sat there in silence for a moment looking out at the empty park they passed by. There wasn't one kid in sight; for that matter, there wasn't anything in the park for kids to play with. Instead of being a playground filled with the laughter of cheerful children, it was diluted with trash and debris everywhere. From a distance it looked as if people were using a section as their own personal dumpster.

"Pull over," Semaj told Sosa, damn near jumping out of the car before Sosa had even stopped.

"Maj!" Sosa said, following right behind her. "What's going on?" she asked, looking around in somewhat of a panic.

Semaj stood on the pavement observing the

neglected park. It was as if something had hit her and the idea of giving back to the community manifested in her heart. "I remember when I was young, I used to sit back and criticize all the rappers from New York that made a lot of money and didn't do shit for the hood," Semaj said, walking over and taking a seat on top of one of the picnic tables. "We gotta do better than them."

Sosa walked over and took a seat right next to her, looking off into the empty park. She'd never seen this side of Semaj before and she was touched by her desire to do better. It showed the growth and maturity in Semaj, and Sosa actually felt a little guilty because she hadn't thought about doing anything for the hood herself. She had it in her mind that it was pointless to try to make a difference, especially in a drug infested neighborhood like Brooklyn.

"So now you wanna save the hood?" Sosa chuckled, pointing to the empty field like it was an impossible task. "You do anything for some people and they will fuck it up," Sosa said, but without the smile that she had on her face before. "Don't forget, I lived in this city for a long time as well, Semaj, and done seen more killings and more violence in two months than most people see in a lifetime."

"Sosa, we are millionaires and we have the opportunity to do something good no matter what other people think or do. And let's not forget that we are the main reason why it looks like this," Semaj said, looking around. "The least that we can do is give back instead of continuing to take away. If not for the hood, then do it to help heal your own soul."

Sosa couldn't even argue with Semaj. Everything that she was saying was the truth. They sold more drugs in New York than anybody else, and the consequences that arrived from it were evident. It could be seen throughout the many neighborhoods that were infested with crack cocaine and powder cocaine.

And it didn't just stop at the drug dealing. Where there are drugs, there is violence, and a constant need for the youth to establish their dominance through violence, which most of the time ended in senseless, countless murders. Semaj knew that story all too well and all she was trying to do was get Sosa to recognize the same thing.

"So what did you have in mind?" Sosa asked, nudging Semaj in her side. "Whatever you wanna do I'll stand behind you one hundred percent."

"Good, because I brought my credit card," Semaj smiled, nudging her back.

Before Sosa could even respond Semaj's phone began to ring. She looked down at it and saw that it was Vikingo calling her again. Semaj was going to answer it but decided against it, being that she didn't feel like dealing with any of the issues that were going on in Colombia. This was a time for relaxation, at least for the first couple of days.

"You better answer that phone before Vikingo kills you," Sosa joked. "You know those Colombians don't play when it comes to their women."

"Shut up girl. Whatever it is, I am sure he can handle it," Semaj shot back. "I'm just tryna enjoy myself for a minute and spend some time with my favorite cousin," she said, jumping up off the table.

They both headed back toward Sosa's car but before Semaj got in, she stopped at the door, turned around, and took one more look at the playground. As she got into the car she pulled her phone out. She already had her mind made up that she was going to take some immediate action and that rebuilding this park was going to be her special little project.

Salina stood in front of the JFK Airport watching taxis and cars pulling up and dropping people off. The loud sound of airplanes flying overhead made it hard for her to even hear Raul calling her. He had to whistle as loud as he could in order to get her attention.

"¡Ven acá!" he yelled, waving at her once she saw him.

"Raul, what's going on? Why am I here?" she asked with an inquisitive look on her face, as though she didn't know what he was about to tell her.

"You gotta go back to Cuba," he said, grabbing her by the arm and pulling her towards the entrance. "There's a flight ..."

"I am not going back to Cuba," she snapped, cutting him off mid-sentence before pulling away from him. "Why do I have to leave?" she asked, with an angry expression on her face.

Previously, Raul had told her about Semaj and how

her grandmother was responsible for their brother's death, but what he failed to mention was the fact that he was planning to kill Semaj because of it.

Salina thought the meeting he'd had with Nikolai and Marco was to see if the Espreilla Family would be removed from their seat in the Tent because Valentina killed their brother without just cause or permission from the rest of the Tent members to do it. If that happened, the Espreilla family would no longer have a seat at the table and Colombia would pretty much be up for grabs. Then, Raul would be able to claim it, just as long as he had land established in Colombia and all of the Tent members agreed to it.

That plan would have been nice if any of it had held any weight, but it didn't, not without Valentina being alive to confront her accusers. That was a right all the members had even if they were dead.

Raul was on some other shit though. Some shit that he didn't want his sister to be a part of, knowing how dangerous it could have been for her. "Listen to me Salina. You cannot be here. It's not safe for you."

"Safe?" What do you mean safe?" she shot back, snatching her arm away from him again. "What are you up to Raul?" she asked, now suspicious of his actions.

Raul grabbed her by the arm, but this time he wasn't leading her into the airport. He pulled her over to the side where there weren't a lot of people walking back and forth by them.

"Look, dis shit got a little deeper than what I had

anticipated. Semaj..."

"What? What about Semaj?" she asked, trying to get Raul to look her in the eyes. "Spit it out," she said through clenched teeth, as she grabbed his cheeks and turned his face to meet hers.

He hesitated for a moment. He didn't know how she was going to react and didn't want to see the look on her face when he tried to explain killing Semaj.

"Semaj got a price on her head and shit is about to get real ugly," he said, looking her in the eyes.

Salina could tell by the look he had on his face that what he was saying wasn't a lie. She put her hand on the top of her head and grabbed a handful of her hair. This was the last thing that she wanted to happen. She had to admit, the death of her brother was wrong. But to kill someone who didn't have anything to do with the murder was also wrong. She didn't care too much about Semaj, but right is right and wrong is wrong, and knowing Raul as good as she did, Salina knew that there was much more to what Raul was telling her.

"Look, I'ma try to fix it," Raul lied, trying to grab a hold of Salina's hand.

Salina knew that was a boldfaced lie, but trying to get the truth out of Raul was almost impossible. She had a feeling that whatever he had going on was going to blow up in his face. Being around when that happened wasn't in Salina's best interest.

"Don't drag our family's name through the mud anymore than it already has been," Salina warned him, before storming off.

Raul put his back up against the wall and watched as his sister disappeared into the airport. He didn't tell her the truth about him being the one who put the hit out on Semaj because he was certain she wouldn't approve. He knew that she didn't have the guts to do what needed to be done, and that was to avenge their brother's death at all costs. Valentina's death by natural causes wasn't going to be the means to end the want for revenge. She only passed her burdens down to the next person that took her place, and that person just so happened to be Semaj.

Sosa and Semaj pulled up to the coffee shop after doing a little shopping and getting a bite to eat. Murda Mitch was sitting in a silver Cadillac DTS across the street from the shop waiting patiently for Semaj. He lifted his head up from texting just in time to see a flaw in her security. It made him get out of his car immediately and walk across the street to check the guards. The closer that he got the angrier he became, because had he been somebody ready to kill Semaj, it wouldn't have been difficult.

Both of her men were sitting in a black Range Rover double-parked behind Sosa's Dodge Challenger. Mitch walked right past them and up to Semaj, who was getting her bags out of the backseat. Sosa had already taken her things into the shop and was having a short conversation with one of her workers.

"Boom, you're dead," Mitch said, as Semaj was

turning around.

She was startled for a second before she recognized who it was. Her two security guards finally exited the car with guns drawn, rushing over, only to be stopped by a wave of Semaj's hand.

"This is who you got watching over you while you're in the city?" Mitch questioned with an attitude, pointing to the two men. "I could have killed you if I wanted to."

"Dad, it's cool," Semaj sighed, trying to calm him down. "I promise you that they will be more on point next time," she assured, looking with a serious face at Willow and Louise, her two guards.

Mitch wasn't buying it. He was still a little hot under the collar, but wasn't going to dig into the situation any deeper and ruin the rest of his day. He had plans to spend some time with his daughter, who was still his best friend, because soon she would be a married woman.

"Are you ready?" Mitch asked Semaj as he continued to grit on her security.

"Yeah, let me just run in and tell Sosa that I am leaving," she said, passing her bags to Louise before running into the coffee shop.

It only took about a minute for her to do that and in a flash she was right back outside, walking side by side with Mitch to his car. Right before they got into the car Mitch paused, looked over and saw Louise and Willow getting into the Range. He slammed his car door and walked back over to the Range Rover. Semaj stood by the passenger side door looking on.

"Don't fuckin' follow us. If this car moves so much as a fuckin' inch when we pull off, I'ma shoot both of ya'll," Mitch yelled out. "I'm her fuckin' security today."

Semaj knew that Mitch was serious when he made that threat, so she just waved at her guards and gave them a glare to tell them that they'd better listen to him. Louis did just that, turning the car off and nodding at Mitch before he walked off. Semaj just shook her head and smiled at her dad and they both got into the car and pulled off.

"Now who in the hell is that?" Agent Davis asked Agent Mason as they both watched through a pair of binoculars.

"Shit, the better question is who are the men with the guns," Mason replied, referring to Louis and Willow, who were still sitting in the Range Rover in front of the coffee shop.

Agent Davis started his investigation immediately, and his target was the coffee shop and the person who Javier thought was the owner, which was Sosa. Today was their first day of staking out and already there was some unusual activity going on that was worth sticking around for.

"Did you get the Cadillac license plate number?" Davis asked.

"Yeah I got it, and the Range Rover and the

Challenger," Mason responded, glancing down at his notepad.

"Good, now run them and see what we get," he directed Mason, before looking back into the binoculars at Sosa getting into her car and pulling off into traffic.

Semaj and Murda Mitch got out of the car at the St. Joseph's cemetery. Semaj thought that it would be nice if they visited Tala's gravesite for a few minutes before they went out. It had been a few years since Tala was murdered, but it seemed like yesterday to Semaj when the two of them were running around the streets together. Although Tala was her Aunt, she and Semaj weren't all that far part in age. So while Tala was taking care of Semaj when they were young, it was like they pretty much grew up together.

"I miss you baby sis," Mitch said, leaning over and grabbing the bottle of Hennessey he kept next to her tombstone. "Remember when she used to take you to the clubs with her? You had to have been about 15 years old at the time." Mitch got a laugh just thinking about it, while taking a swig of the Hennessey.

"Yeah, most of the time it was to set a nigga up. She was vicious wit it," Semaj smiled. "Can you imagine what she would be like if she was still alive?"

"That girl would have been a problem," Mitch said, shaking his head, taking another swig of the bottle and passing it to Semaj.

They both just sat there and reminisced about all of the good old days and how much fun they had. It had been a long road for Semaj and Mitch, but if they had any idea what was in store for them in the near future, they would come to realize that their journey in life was just about to begin.

Penny sat in the car looking through her rearview mirror on 125th Street waiting for Qua to show up. She reached over and grabbed her phone, seeing that somebody was sending her a text. She looked and saw it was Sosa letting her know that she was back at the coffee shop and telling her to call whenever it was convenient. Penny was two seconds away from calling her back when she took a second look in her rearview and saw Qua's Benz coming down the narrow street doing about 5 miles an hour. His car pulled in and parked right behind Penny, but when the door opened, it wasn't Qua that got out of the car, it was Ron, Qua's right hand man.

"Where's ya boy?" she asked, getting out of the all-white Mustang.

"He couldn't make it. He said that he had some shit to take care of," Ron answered. "Don't worry about it Ma. I got da bread. So do you got da shit wit you?" he asked, leaning up against her car.

"Naw playboy. That's not how it works. This right here is like a pre-meeting where you pass off the money and then wait on my phone call to tell you where to pick the work up from."

"Ma, you must be crazy if you think that I'm about to give you my bread without you having the product right here," Ron said, looking over at her like she was crazy.

"See, this is why he should have come instead of you. Tell Qua to call me when he's not doing shit," Penny said, opening the driver's side door to get back in her car and leave.

"Hold up," Ron responded, whipping out his phone to call Qua.

This definitely wasn't the way that he did business and he really wasn't feeling it. He didn't even know Penny like that, or Sosa for that matter.

"Yo, what up son?" Qua answered, seeing who it was that was calling him.

"Yo, Shorty said that she want the money before she give up the pussy, dog," Ron spoke in riddles.

"Yeah man, she is a high-priced whore. You gotta pay before you get laid messing around with her. But don't worry, dat pussy good son and it's worth the wait," Qua responded, pretty much letting Ron know that it was okay to give her the money.

It wasn't like Qua didn't know where to find Sosa if something went wrong with the money. Besides, he knew Sosa well enough to know that she of all people wouldn't try to beat anybody for their money. This was just her way of doing business, something he couldn't knock, especially if it was going to keep somebody out of jail.

"Yo ma, my bad. Qua said it was cool," Ron said, walking back to his car and grabbing the duffle bag. "Yo, don't take dis shit personal. It's just business, you know," Ron said, walking over to her and handing her the bag.

"It's no hard feelings baby-boy. I probably would have done the same thing if I was you," she said, tossing the money into the backseat. "Tell Qua I'ma call him in an hour with the location."

"Are you going to be there?" Ron asked, with a grin on his face.

The more that he looked at Penny, the sexier she was becoming to him. There was something about the way she carried herself that was turning him on, plus she had a crazy body and a cute face to match. But her "I don't give a fuck" attitude was what turned him on the most.

"Yeah, I will be there," she said, with a flirtatious smirk on her face as she got back into the car.

Ron stood there and watched her pull off down the street. "I'ma fuck da shit out of you," he mumbled to himself before walking back to his car.

Chapter 7

"Get da fuck outta here," Ron mumbled to himself looking at the red and blue lights flashing in his rearview mirror.

He damn near choked on the weed smoke as he quickly tried to put the blunt out before he actually pulled his car over to the side. Every last one of his windows were down in an instant and the air conditioner blasted a strong, citrus scent through the vents, giving the car a new smell. A couple of minutes went by before the two cops got out of their car and walked up to his black Nissan Maxima. When Ron looked up, he was taken by surprised when he saw the man standing before him had on a suit. He looked over out of the passenger side window and saw that the other cop was also suited.

"What's up Ronald?" Agent Davis greeted, lowering his head so that he could see inside the car.

Agent Davis really wasn't sure if that was his name, but took a shot in the dark since the name that the car was registered to was Ronald Graham. Ron pretty much confirmed it by the look of surprise on his face when he heard his name.

"What can I do for you this evening, officer?" Ron asked, looking up at Agent Davis.

"Do I look like a fucking officer to you?" Agent David arrogantly asked.

Ron looked into his rearview and saw that the red and blue lights were only flashing from the headlights and not from the roof. He didn't know whether or not the car was a Crown Victoria or a Grand Marquis, but what he did know was that they were either detectives or the feds.

"You know, I have a nose like a hound," Agent Davis said, sticking his head inside of the window.

"I can smell grass a mile away and in my 15 years of doin' this shit, I would bet the house that you got something in this car that you are not supposed to have," he said, reaching over and grabbing the keys out of the ignition.

Ron leaned his head on the headrest and closed his eyes. All he could think about was the gun he had under his seat and the three bricks of cocaine, along with a brick of crack he had in his stash spot. His heart was racing, but he kept his cool knowing that it would take more than the average search to find the cocaine. The gun on the other hand, was something he might have had to bite.

"I'm going to need you to step out of the car," Agent Davis said, opening the driver's door.

Ron did what he was ordered to do, stepping out of the car. He was handcuffed immediately for security purposes and was placed at the back of the car while Davis began to search. Mason stood right behind Ron in case he tried to run.

"I hope you got probable cause to search my vehicle," Ron scoffed, trying to throw around a few legal terms he learned while he was in jail.

Davis pulled himself back out of the car after hearing that. He inhaled deeply through his nose and then exhaled.

"I smell marijuana. Do you smell that, partner?" Davis asked, looking at Agent Mason.

"Yeah, it smells like purple haze," Mason answered, tapping Ron on his back.

"Well there is ya probable cause, smart ass," Davis said, as he began reaching back into the car.

He rambled around for a while in the back seat and made his way up to the front. Ron looked at him through the back window the whole time, watching him pass by the stash spot several times. The first time Davis reached under the driver side seat, he didn't feel anything. He dug a little deeper and felt around a little more thoroughly until he felt the butt of the gun poking out from the top of the seat.

"Awwweeee, what do we have here?" Davis said, pulling the large .45 Ruger out from under the seat.

Ron didn't say a word. He just kept watching as Davis continued his search of the car. He already prepared himself for that so there was no surprise when it happened. It was the other shit that he had in the car that would have become a problem if it were found. Davis would never be able to find the coke under these circumstances though. The stash spot was too high-tech for him to crack the code to get in.

With that, Davis wore himself out before he could find anything else in the car, and finally gave up. By the time that he was done, the sweat from his underarms had made stains on his shirt. He swore that there was more in the car, so much so that the search was going to continue, but this time it was going to happen somewhere where he had access to some tools.

"Put him in the back seat. He is going for a ride," Davis told his partner as he walked to the back of the car wiping the sweat from his forehead.

Ron smiled as he was being led to the unmarked car by Agent Mason. He knew that the minute he got bail he'd be right back on the streets within the hour. It wasn't until he heard Davis standing outside by the Maxima calling for a flatbed tow truck that Ron became concerned and actually started to sweat a little himself.

"Let me call you back," Sosa said, hanging up the phone and getting up from her table in the back of the coffee shop.

She was shocked to see Santos, her unofficial boyfriend, walking through the door and taking a seat at the table next to the window. This was the first time that he had been to the shop, so it caught Sosa by surprise to see him. She started to creep off and slide into her office but Santos made eye contact with her, making it impossible for her to avoid him.

"Can I get you something?" a waitress asked, walking over to Santos with a pen and a notepad in her hand.

"Yeah, bring us over a couple cups of tea," he responded, watching Sosa walk across the room towards him.

The waitress looked to see who he was looking at and raised one eyebrow when she noticed Sosa headed in their direction. There was an awkward moment of silence before Sosa dismissed the waitress.

"What are you doing here, Santos?" Sosa asked, in a semi-whining tone. "I thought we agreed…you know."

"Yeah, I know. I was just in the neighborhood and thought that I would take a look at where you work," Santos said, pulling an extra chair out from the table for her to take a seat.

Sosa kind of felt bad lying to Santos' face and telling him that she worked at a coffee shop. She did that a while back when she first met him and never took the time to come clean with the truth. She still didn't know why she had lied to him in the first place. The coffee shop was the first thing that had come to mind when he asked her, and ever since then she had been riding with that story. That was over four months ago.

Her reason for doing it was personal. She had a lot of trust issues and wasn't sure that telling him she was the biggest drug dealer in New York was the best thing to do.

"Sit down," Santos said, with a serious look on his face. "I need to talk to you about something."

"Can't this wait until later on?" Sosa asked, looking around the coffee shop at the few nosy people sitting around peeking over at her.

It was kind of embarrassing having him there. Nobody had ever seen Sosa talking to a man before, outside of the business aspect of her life. Her personal life was like a mystery to everybody and that's the way she liked it. Santos was trying his best to break that barrier and it was starting to show. He answered her last question with a simple nod of his head in the direction of the empty chair. Sosa complied, grabbing the chair and taking a seat.

"I gotta get back to work," she lied.

He just smiled; already having done his homework on Sosa, he knew that she wasn't an employee, but rather the owner of the shop. "Babe."

"Don't call me that in here," Sosa checked him, looking around the room to see if anybody had heard him say that.

"Well, Samantha," he said, shrugging his shoulders, "I'm really feeling you and I want you to know that you don't ever have to lie to me, nor do you ever have to worry about me hurting you," he said, looking her in her eyes.

"What are you talking about?" she said, breaking

his eye contact. "I know all that, Santos."

Actually, Sosa had stronger feelings for Santos than what he knew. She never admitted it to him but she cared for him deeply; she wasn't really sure if he felt the same about her. That was the main reason why she wasn't so open in public with their relationship. Until she knew that he was going to be around for the long haul, her plans were to stay low-key with it. But again, Santos was trying to break that wall in their relationship. He was tired of not being able to show his affection towards her the way that he would like to.

"Listen to me Samantha, I'm going to be very clear, so that you understand what I am about to tell you."

Sosa sat up and was attentive. It kind of sounded like he was about to break up with her, but it was the total opposite. He reached across the table and put his hands over hers. She started to pull away from him but something about the way Santos looked at her made her stop.

"We been at this for over four months now, and I know this might be early for me to say, but I gotta keep it 100 wit' you. I'm in love with you, Samantha," he confessed, rubbing his thumb against the back of her hand.

Sosa instinctively looked to her left and then to her right to see if anybody had heard him. She pulled her hand from under his right before the waitress walked up and placed the two glasses of tea on the table. Sosa didn't say anything the whole time the waitress was there.

"What makes you think that you love me Santos?" Sosa asked, with a confused look on her face. "We barely know each other."

"Let me tell you one thing about love. It don't have an established time when it decides to manifest. It can hit you whenever it feels like it," Santos said, reaching over and grabbing her hand.

Sosa didn't know how to take it. Throughout her whole life, no man had ever professed his love for her in the manner in which Santos did. Ox was the closest thing to love Sosa had ever experienced, and even then, he never came out and verbally admitted that he loved her. Hearing Santos say it was kind of confusing, but heartfelt. She couldn't tell whether he was genuine with how he felt though. The crazy part about it was that Sosa thought for a moment that she was in love with him too.

"Right now ain't the time or the place for this conversation, babe." She looked around to see if anybody heard her call him that. "I promise you that as soon as I leave here tonight I'ma come right over to your house to finish this conversation," Sosa told him.

Santos didn't put up a fight in the least. He could see the sincerity in her eyes and knew that he could expect to see her tonight. He let her hand go, took a sip of the tea on the table and then got up. He thought about leaning over and kissing her on the forehead but decided against it. He did something he knew would have a better effect on her. He stood behind her and put his hand on her shoulder, then rubbed his thumb across the side of her neck. That was Sosa's spot and the only thing that she could do was smile from the sensation it gave her. "I'll see you tonight," he said, before walking off towards the front door.

Ron didn't even make it to the police station messing around with Agent Davis. They took him straight to the police impound where he watched as his car was brought in on the flatbed and lowered onto the ground. A few minutes later a K-9 unit pulled in, getting every bit of Ron's attention as he sat in a chair off to the side of the garage. The dog immediately started barking in the back seat of the patrol car before the door even opened. Davis smiled as he opened up all of the Nissan Maxima doors, knowing from experience that the dog picked up the scent of drugs.

He looked over at Ron who had the dumbest look on his face that told the tall tale of his guilt. As soon as his handler let him out of the patrol car, the dog went straight to work. He bit and scratched up the back seats like he was trying to get a buried t-bone steak. The handler pulled him out of the car so that the mechanics could do their part.

"This shit ain't looking good for you at all," Agent Davis said, walking over and taking a seat next to Ron. "I know that you got a stash spot somewhere in the back seat. It may take us a while but we are going to find it. Now, if you make it easy on yourself and crack it open for me, I might be able to work with you," Davis said, tossing a floor mat he had from the car to the side.

Ron thought about it for a split second but ultimately came to the conclusion that he wasn't going to make things easier for the Agents, knowing that at the end of all of this, he was going to jail any fuckin' way. He was going to make them work tonight. The mechanics had tried just about everything that they could to get to a small compartment on the right side of the back seat. It took a little over 3 hours and over four mechanics to get the stash spot to unlock, but they finally did it.

"Jackpot!" Mason yelled from inside of the car, reaching in and grabbing one of the kilos of cocaine.

He tossed it over to Davis who was still sitting next to Ron. The coke was so strong he could smell it through the wrapper. The dog, who was back in the patrol car, was going crazy from the strong odor.

"Damn, boy. This some strong shit," Davis cracked, holding the kilo in front of him. "How much of this shit is back there?" he yelled out to Mason.

"It's two more of those and it looks like some cooked up stuff in another package, possibly another whole kilo," Mason explained.

"Whoaaaa! Now that is a lot of shit," Agent Davis taunted, tossing the kilo that he had in his hand back to Mason.

He reached into his back pocket, pulled out his cell phone and began dialing numbers. Ron watched as Davis walked across the room and took a seat on the trunk of the Maxima. The phone conversation was brief, but when he hung up, Davis had a smile on his face.

"Now look Mr. Tucker, I'm going to run down some numbers for you and after I am done we can talk," Davis said, hopping down off the trunk and walking back over to Ron. "First and foremost, this is officially a federal investigation, meaning you will be punished in accordance to the federal law, not the state. You have three kilos of cocaine and probably a whole kilo of crack over there," Davis said, looking over his shoulder at the kilos and the gun sitting on the hood of the car. You're looking at a mandatory minimum of 10 years for the crack by itself and about another 5 years for the powder. The gun also has a mandatory minimum of 5 years behind it and it must run consecutive to the drugs. Now here is the kicker," Davis smiled, rubbing his hands together with a devious grin on his face. "You got a vicious background. I mean, felonies out the ass. Two prior convictions for drugs plus this one will put you at a mandatory life sentence, guaranteed."

Davis went so far as to Google the federal statute on his phone so that Ron could read it for himself, which he did out of curiosity. Everything that Davis said was written in black and white, all the way down to the life sentence that he threatened him with.

"Now that you know what you're facing, let me tell you the flipside to this coin," Davis continued. "I am in a position where I can make all of this go away. You haven't been charged as of yet and I can easily take those cuffs off of you and put you right back out onto the streets. Nobody would even know that you were here."

"Yeah, how much is that gonna cost me?" Ron asked, sitting up in his chair.

Nothing came free in this world and Ron knew it. The feds were probably the dirtiest law officials in America, so the Catch-22 was already in effect the moment that Ron's car was pulled over. Not only was Agent Davis watching the coffee shop, he was also watching Penny. He was able to do surveillance for the first meeting Ron and Penny had when they established the money aspect of the deal, but he was unable to catch the second meeting when the drugs were exchanged. Knowing that he had missed out on the second and, most important meeting, Davis put Ron under surveillance too and waited for the right time to catch him slipping. He did, and that's what got Ron to this point right here and right now.

The next words that would come out of Davis' mouth would be the words that would change Ron's life. They were the kind of words that would separate the boys from the men, the weak from the strong. These were the kind of words that would determine if you were built for the game or if you would be killed in the streets.

"I want you to work for me. I want you to give up your connect and in return I will give you back your freedom," Davis offered. "Now before you answer that I need you to understand that this is a one-time offer. Once I book you, there are no more negotiations," he warned.

Ron sat there in silence looking at the coke on the hood of the car and thinking about the life sentence that he had just read about. Then Ron thought about his reputation in the hood and how much of a G he was. He never folded under pressure no matter what kind of odds he was facing. He would never feel right working with the authorities, but at the same time, he couldn't ignore the possibility of spending the rest of his life in prison for a drug charge. Either way, he had to make a choice, and Davis wasn't making it any easier standing over him like he was somebody's pops. He looked at Davis, then at Agent Mason and then at the gun on the trunk. He made the choice that most men would have made in this predicament. He stood up, walked to the back of Davis's car and leaned against the door.

Sosa pulled into Santos's apartment complex and parked. She sat in the car before going into the building just so she could process everything that was about to be put on the table for discussion. She couldn't believe how deep the relationship between her and Santos had gotten over the course of four months. It started out as just a means for Sosa to relieve some sexual stress. He was only a boy toy, then one thing led to another and Sosa found herself not just wanting Santos, but in a sense needing him.

It wasn't like Santos was a bad guy, either. He used to be in the streets real heavy, but after doing 8 years up State he made some critical changes in his life, one being getting a job and another, leaving the drug game alone. That alone was a plus in Sosa's eyes. The time that she did spend with him was like the balance in her life she really needed. He lived a basic life. No partying, no drugs, a little bit of alcohol on occasion, and he kept strong ties to the hood, which meant his swag was still up to date. He wasn't rich and he didn't live an extravagant lifestyle, nor was he broke and struggling with the everyday hustle. He was the kind of nigga most females dreamed of being with, but at the same time, Sosa wasn't like most females.

"Come on Sosa, you can't fall in love now," she mumbled to herself, tapping on the steering wheel.

After about 15 minutes of sitting in the car contemplating how she was going to approach the situation, she opened the car door and headed towards the building. The only thing she could think about the whole time walking into the building was Santos telling her that he was in love with her. This conversation was going to be more difficult then she thought, but she was ready to deal with it head on.

Chapter 8

A knock at the hotel room door woke Semaj out of her sleep. She looked over at her cell phone for the time, and before she could put her head back down on the pillow the knocking on the door continued. She jumped up with a major attitude and stormed to the door. When she flung the door open, Roberto, her security was standing there.

"Ms. Espreilla, I am sorry to bother you," he stuttered.

"No, its fine Roberto, what's wrong?" she questioned, as she stood behind the door.

"I just got a call from Colombia and they said Vikingo had been shot."

Semaj thought that she might have still been asleep and misheard what Roberto had said. "What did you say?" she asked, sticking her head out a little further to make sure she understood every word.

"I said that Vikingo's been shot. He's in the hospital."

Semaj immediately darted from behind the door and across the room to retrieve her cell. Roberto had to turn his head and close the door, seeing that all she had on was her bra and panties. She tried to call Vikingo's phone but it went straight to voicemail twice before her cell went dead.

"What the hell is going on?" she said to herself digging in her suitcase for a pair of jeans and a shirt.

"Roberto! Roberto!" she yelled, running back to the door.

"Si, Señorita," he answered, walking back down the hallway to her room.

"I want you to get somebody on the phone right now who can tell me what's going on," she demanded.

Paulette stood in front of the window of her hotel room looking down at Lower Manhattan. She was completely intrigued by what she had seen of the city so far, especially the tall buildings posted up everywhere.

"So dis is why you like New York City so much," Paulette mumbled to herself out loud, thinking about her brother Ox.

He'd spent a great deal of time and done a lot of business in the city, and Paulette could remember him always telling her that she needed to come there if she wanted to experience some of the finer things in life. She used to wave him off and tell him that there was no place like Jamaica. Paulette was right in a sense. Jamaica was unique, but New York had much more to offer.

"I just talked to Dominic," Doc announced, coming through the door. "He got something for us but we gotta be there in an hour," he said, walking over and grabbing the spliff out of the ashtray.

Before anything else could happen, Paulette and Patrick desperately needed to get some firearms. They really couldn't move without them, and weren't even going to try and attempt to, knowing and hearing all of the stories about how violent New York could be. Paulette wanted to increase her chances of successfully extracting Nyala out of the city, instead of getting herself killed before she got the chance to. Plus, she had some unfinished business with Sosa that needed to be settled before she left the States.

"Call Dominic back and tell 'em we're on our way right now," Paulette said, walking away from the window.

She grabbed her keys and bag off the table and headed out the door. She was in such a hurry to get strapped that Doc didn't have time to enjoy the weed he was about to light up.

Semaj paced back and forth in her room listening to Maria try and explain everything she knew about the shooting, which obviously wasn't much considering the fact that she wasn't there. All she heard, and this was from the workers, was that poachers had shot him. What she did know and explained to Semaj was the condition of Vikingo, which was critical. He had lost a lot of blood and the bullet did some extensive damage to his back. He went into a coma right after the first surgery and doctors weren't sure if he was going to come out of it.

Semaj finally took a seat on the bed after hanging up the phone once Maria was done explaining the situation to her. She put her head down and dragged her fingers through her hair in a stressful manner. She couldn't muster the thought of how bold the poachers had become and why Vikingo had to be the one to suffer behind it. Semaj snapped, kicking the nightstand over in frustration.

"Señorita!" Roberto yelled out, knocking on the door. "Is everything alright?"

She walked over to the door and opened it. Roberto could see the stress in her eyes. "Get us on the next thing smoking back home," she instructed.

Semaj had only been in the city for 24 hours and now she was headed right back home. As much as she was starting to enjoy being back in the city with family and friends, her second home was in need of her leadership right now. Vikingo's tragedy outweighed everything else at the moment.

Let me hear you say it," Santos said, pushing his dick deeper into Sosa's dripping wet insides.

She looked back at her ass smacking up against his lower abdomen with every stroke he took. Holding onto the headboard for support, Sosa threw every inch of her body on him letting Santos know that she could take it.

"No!" she yelled out between the moans of pleasure, refusing to say what he wanted to hear.

The strokes only got deeper and more intense as the sound of Sosa's ass cheeks clapping filled the bedroom. He was determined to make her say it. "Let me hear you," he demanded in an authoritative yet persuasive voice, as he pounded away without losing any stamina.

"I'm cumming! " Sosa cried out through grunts.

That wasn't what he wanted to hear, but the warm moist sensation of her cum oozing out of her pussy and lathering his dick like a lubricant almost made him shoot a load off himself. It wasn't happening though. He took a deep breath and pushed his nut back down into his balls. He wasn't going to cum until he got what he wanted.

"I know what you want," he said, pulling his dick out and flipping Sosa onto her back.

He slid his 10 inch pleasure stick right back inside of her, this time slowing things down a little. The only way he could hit Sosa's spot and get her to do pretty much whatever he said was if she was laying missionary, her favorite position. There was something about a man dominating her by being on top, fucking her face-to-face, that made Sosa totally submissive.

"Say it," he said softly, leaning in and kissing her gently.

Sosa could feel the top of his dick tapping up against her back wall with every stroke. He felt hypnotically good inside of her, so much that Sosa could feel herself reaching her climax, again.

"Este gatito le pertenece a usted, papa," Sosa whispered into Santo's ear.

A big smile came over his face. Those were the words he wanted to hear, and the way that Sosa said them was the ultimate high. He leaned in and kissed her again, thrusting his manhood deeper inside of her. He could feel himself about to cum and Sosa could feel it too. The deep slow strokes, the heavy breathing and the feeling of his body pressed against hers were the perfect combination for the ultimate orgasm.

"Si, bebé! Te quiero!" Sosa moaned, holding onto his back.

Santo was going to pull out when he busted but Sosa grabbed his waist and pushed him back in. She wanted to feel it inside of her and that's exactly what he gave her. His thick, warm cum shot out of his dick, filling her insides with every drop. Sosa exploded to, drenching his tool with a thin coat of her own fluids.

"Don't write checks ya ass can't cash," Santos said, referring to Sosa wanting him to cum inside of her.

Sosa just smiled. Before she could respond to his comment, her cell phone almost vibrated off the nightstand. She couldn't ignore it. Nyala was at her friend's sleepover and Sosa had to be on point in case she wanted to come home. She grabbed the phone and saw the unfamiliar number on her screen.

"Hold on, I gotta take this," she said, putting her finger up to Santos' lips. "Yeah, whasup?" she answered with her legs still spread apart for Santos.

His dick was still rock hard so he kept stroking lightly as she continued talking on the phone.

"Yo, there's a problem. I gotta go back to Colombia," Semaj said into the phone, getting Sosa's full, undivided attention.

"What's going on Maj?" Sosa asked, hearing the seriousness in her voice.

"Vikingo got shot by a poacher and he's in the hospital," Semaj explained, as she was checking out of the hotel.

Sosa sat up in the bed so fast she bent Santos' dick before releasing her grasp. "What do you need me to do?"

"Nothing. really. I just needed you to know what was going on."

"You need me to come with you?" Sosa asked, then catching the crazy look Santos had on his face after hearing her volunteer.

"I'm already on my way to the airport. Besides, I still gotta come back in a few days for the 16 Tent meeting."

Sosa had damn near forgotten about the meeting being scheduled for New York this time, and it was a good thing Semaj reminded her because she was supposed to be hosting it.

"Listen, you call me when you touch down in Colombia and if you need me for anything don't hesitate to call," Sosa said, before they both hung up.

"I know Javier didn't randomly pick this place out to drop cocaine off. And it damn sure wasn't a coincidence that Ron said he bought 100 kilos from somebody that works there either," Agent Davis said to his partner as they sat in an unmarked car two blocks away from the coffee shop.

"So what? Are we gonna just sit here and wait?" Mason asked, with a bit of frustration in his voice.

Too much attention had been drawn to the coffee shop for Davis to ignore. First, it was Javier trying to deliver 200 kilos, then it was Semaj's armed guards sitting in front of the place, then Penny on a side street meeting up with Ron, and now Ron getting caught with three bricks of powder and one brick of crack and saying he got it from the shop.

In court it would be a lot of circumstantial evidence. Lawyers call them holes, because if they arrested everybody right now, the only thing that they would have was the cocaine they took off Ron. Even if he testified and said the coke came from Penny and the coffee shop, there was nothing else to substantiate his claim. It would be his word against everybody else's, and being that he was a convicted felon facing the rest of his life in prison, it would be hard for any juror to believe that he was telling the truth. Bottom line, neither Ron nor Javier were worth Jack shit right now until Ron could get some stronger evidence to help make the case.

"We don't even know who Sosa is," Mason said, looking out of his window at the heavy flow of people walking past the car.

"More than likely it's a man, possibly Spanish or descendant of Spanish. I am telling you Mason, I got a good feeling about this," Davis said, picking up the binoculars and looking down the street.

From experience Mason knew that if Davis had a strong feeling about something, 9 times out of 10 he was going to be right about it. There was nothing else Mason could do but sit back and enjoy the ride, which definitely was going to be a long one if they thought that bringing Sosa down was going to be easy.

I wonder what agency you guys are from. Penny thought to herself as she snapped a few pictures of the unmarked car Davis and Mason were in.

Penny was paid to be on point like a sniper, so when she made her rounds this morning before opening the coffee shop, she spotted what she thought was two cops a block and a half away looking in the direction of the store. One was looking through a set of binoculars while the other periodically took a few pictures. Penny just decided to take a few pictures of her own and the morning rush hour traffic was the perfect cover for her. It was almost impossible for the Agents to notice Penny while hundreds of people walked past their car, some speed-walking while others strolled. She stood a mere 15 feet away snapping pics with her cell phone. Once she got the license plate number, make and model of the car, she faded off into the heavy flow of traffic unnoticed.

Chapter 9

Semaj found herself jogging through the small Colombian hospital looking for Vikingo's room. Her security was right on her trail. A small group of members were sitting outside of Vikingo's room when she made her way down the hall. Her heart was racing. She didn't know what she was about to walk in on, and when she finally made it to the room it was clear that Vikingo was in bad shape. Long faces and an abundance of tears proved that.

Several family members stepped to the side, allowing Semaj to enter the room. Maria was there standing next to his bed holding his hand. The numerous tubes and cables running in and out of his body broke Semaj down. Her legs got too weak to hold her up and before she could make it to his bedside, she dropped to her knees. Maria had to come over and help her back to her feet before anybody in the hallway noticed, especially the two police that had driven Vikingo to the hospital. Any sign of weakness was bad for someone of Semaj's stature.

"Señorita, come on," Maria said, lifting her to her feet.

Semaj had to pull herself together, realizing wolves could be lurking in the wings. She was the head of the family and everybody looked up to her for strength.

"Vikingo," Semaj sniveled, finally being able to look down at his badly injured body. She wanted to release a full fledge of tears so badly, but she couldn't. "Go and get a doctor," she told Maria. She didn't have to go far because a doctor was already coming into the room.

"Hola te pierdas. Desafortunadamente..."

"English!" Semaj barked, cutting him off.

Her brain was too fried to be trying to translate shit. Luckily the doctor knew English well enough to honor her request. "He has sustained a lot of damage and lost a lot of blood. I don't know..."

The doctor hesitated for a second. "What?" Semaj shot back, trying to look him in the eyes.

"This is a good hospital but we don't have... uh... how do I say dis...the right technology here to help him," the doctor admitted.

"So what are you saying, doctor?" Semaj spit with an attitude. "You sayin' the hospital is gonna let him die?" she snapped.

"I am sorry, but there is nothing else we can do," the doctor responded.

Semaj looked over at Vikingo. There was no way she was going let him die in this hospital. She got to thinking real hard. There was one hospital that she knew for sure could put Vikingo back together. A hospital that had the best technology money could buy. She grabbed a hold of the doctor's arm before he walked out the door.

"Is it safe for him to fly?" she asked the doctor, and then looked over at Vikingo.

Paulette pulled up in front of Little Rock Elementary school just after 12:00 in the afternoon. Some kids were playing in the schoolyard, but she could tell by the age group that Nyala wasn't one of them. She reached into her bag and grabbed a chrome .380, cocking it back and putting a bullet into the chamber. She had no intentions of using the gun, but in the event that it became necessary, having it was better than regretting not having it if things didn't go as planned.

The school wasn't that big so finding the main office was easy once she made it into the building. Kids were running around everywhere and Paulette only wished that she'd run into Nyala so she wouldn't have to go through the process of finding out where in the school she would be.

"Good afternoon," the secretary greeted her at the front desk.

Although it was out of her character, Paulette put on a smile and spoke in a respectable manner to avoid any suspicion. Her accent was the only thing that she couldn't hide.

"Hello, I came to pick up my niece a little early today. Could you tell me what class she is in right now?" Paulette asked, pulling her long, thick dreadlocks to one side of her shoulder.

"Well, what's your niece's name?" the secretary asked, looking at the computer screen with her hands on the keyboard.

Paulette wasn't sure if Sosa had changed Nyala's name because she'd had the same last name as Ox, so she had no other choice but to try. "Her name is Nyala Gambles," Paulette said, placing her purse on the table.

The name Nyala Gambles wasn't showing up in the computer. "Are you sure you have the right name, because we do not have a Nyala Gambles in this school," the secretary said, scrolling down a list of names.

Paulette looked off for a second. She was trying to think of Sosa's real name, thinking Nyala probably was under her name. Then it hit her. The information that the private investigator gave her had all of Nyala's information on it. She reached into her bag and moved some papers around before pulling out Nyala's school records. She couldn't believe that she hadn't thought of this before.

"Milano. I am sorry, her name is Nyala Milano," Paulette corrected herself and smiled again, trying to do damage control.

It was a little too late because Paulette could see that the secretary's entire demeanor had changed. She punched the name into the computer anyway, and saw that Nyala was in class 204. The secretary looked back up at Paulette. She didn't look too much like a threat, but the recent massacre at Sandy Hook Elementary and the kidnapping of a child from an elementary school in Philadelphia had all schools on high alert.

"Just give me a second," the secretary told Paulette as she picked up the phone.

Paulette thought that she was about to call the cops. A speedy exit was the only way out and that's exactly what was going to happen, that is until an older, white, gray-headed woman stuck her head out of one of the offices and waved for Paulette.

"I am sorry, but it's policy that we get clearance from the Principal to release any of our students," the secretary tried to explain before Paulette walked off and headed towards the Principal's office.

The Principal stepped to the side and let Paulette in. "I apologize for any inconvenience, but we have certain precautions set in place to try and guarantee the safety of our students, as that is our first priority," the Principal said, taking a seat behind her desk. "Now what is your relation to Nyala?"

"She's my niece."

"Well, before I release her to your care, we're going to have to call her mother to confirm that information."

"That won't be necessary." Paulette shot back, now becoming a little irritated. "Her mother knows I am here. Just let me know what classroom she is in," Paulette somewhat demanded.

Principal Taylor could see that something wasn't right. She wasn't about to let some stranger come in and take one of her students out of school, especially without the parent's permission. She took pride in her job and there wasn't about to be a preventable tragedy in her school on her watch.

"Well, I won't be releasing her to you without the parent's permission," the Principal made clear, getting up from her desk in an attempt to escort Paulette out of her office.

Paulette jumped up too, only to stop her at the side of her desk. She was tired of playing games with all the apologies and policies. She reached into her bag and pulled out the .380, placing it down by her side. Shockingly, the presence of the gun didn't faze Ms. Taylor at all. She even walked up closer to Paulette just to let her know that she wasn't scared.

"You shoot me, the school police will be here within seconds," Principal Taylor informed her.

Paulette scanned the room in the blink of an eye. She knew that she couldn't let the Principal just leave the office. Paulette would be arrested before she exited the building, and going to jail wasn't an option for her right now. Paulette slowly put the gun back into her purse knowing that the blast from the gun would draw a lot of unwanted attention .

"You should have let me take her," Paulette said, before reaching over and grabbing the thick, heavy plaque off the principle's desk.

By the time Principle Taylor looked over to see what it was she had grabbed, Paulette was already in the motion of swinging it. The award cracked Ms. Taylor on the side of her temple. Blood squirted out of her head like a water fountain. The blow knocked her out instantly and if it weren't for Paulette catching her before her body hit the ground, it would have made enough noise to get the peoples' attention outside of the office.

Paulette walked the body around to the back of her desk and laid it on the floor. She had blood all over her shirt and knew there was no way she could leave the office unnoticed. She went to the door and cracked it open slightly to look into the hallway. The secretary was at her desk attending to another woman. "Bumba clot!" she mumbled to herself, closing the office door. She didn't know how she was going to make it out of the building but she knew she had to do something quick, fast, and in a hurry.

"Right this way, Señorita," Sergeant Gonzalez said, leading Semaj into the warehouse.

Gonzalez was one of the many crooked cops in Colombia whom Semaj had on her payroll. He was loyal to the Espreilla Family and had been since the time Valentina was alive. When he and his team ran into Semaj's warehouse after Vikingo was shot, they killed all of the four gunmen but one. Gonzalez kept him alive for this very reason. When Semaj walked into the warehouse, she noticed the dead bodies were still there lying in pools of blood. The scene was gruesome, but Semaj showed no weakness as she stepped over the bodies to get to the man that was still alive.

He was sitting in a chair with his hands tied behind him. Blood covered his shirt from the beating Gonzalez had given him before she'd gotten there. "¿Cuál es su nombre? " Semaj asked, wanting to know his name. "¿Cuál es tu maldito nombre?" she roared, backhanding him across the face.

"Fuck you!" He spit a glob of blood at her. She jumped back but it still got on her leg, staining her cream khakis. Gonzalez swiftly hit him in his jaw with the butt of his rifle, almost knocking him out.

"Why are you poaching on my land?" Semaj spoke in English, since he could obviously understand and speak it. She slowly walked around and stood behind him.

"That's 'cause he's not a poacher, Señorita," Gonzalez said. "These men are guerrillas. They work for a cartel," he said, waving his rifle at the dead men on the floor.

"Guerrillas?" Semaj asked, grabbing a handful of the man's hair and pulling his head back. "Why the fuck are guerrillas sitting in my warehouse and what cartel would be stupid enough to try me?" she shouted out, looking around the room at everybody.

Guerrillas coming through your establishment meant one thing and one thing only, and that was to let you know your time was up. Sending this few members was considered a warning. Next time, Semaj could expect 100 or better running down on the compound with large assault rifles, killing everything that breathed.

"Who sent you?" Semaj yelled, pushing the man's head forward.

He just sat there and started laughing at Semaj. "Usted es debil. No eres Valentina," the man continued to laugh. He had just told Semaj that she was weak and that she was no Valentina. "Tienes 24 horas para abandonar esta tierra a menos que quieras morir," the man threatened.

Semaj looked at him like he was crazy. Who in their right mind would be so bold as to be giving Semaj 24 hours to leave her land? The Espreilla Family was the second largest family in Colombia. They were more feared and made more money than any of the many cartels in Colombia.

"You got one more fuckin' chance to tell me who sent you or you will die in less than that same 24 hours you gave me," Semaj said, pulling a Glock .40 from her back waist to let the motherfucker know she wasn't bluffing.

"Me matas hoy voy a verte en el infierno de manana," the man taunted Semaj with sinister laughter, telling Semaj that if she killed him today, he would see her in hell tomorrow.

"Have it your way." Semaj turned to Gonzalez. "Kill this bastard, but torture his ass to death. I'm talkin' 'bout slicing one body part off at a time starting with his fingers until you chop off his balls. If he's able to survive though that torture without dying, make sure you rip off his ears and tongue last so he can hear himself scream out in agony," Semaj ordered, then bent down and stared into the man's dark eyes. "You gon' learn today what happens when you fuck wit' Semaj. And no you won't be seeing me in hell. I run this town. Colombia belongs to me, bitch!"

"When you finish with him, drop all their bodies off into the city," Semaj instructed Gonzalez, and then left the warehouse.

Sosa pulled up to the Little Rock Elementary School and cops were everywhere. Her heart started racing and she damn near went into a panic attack. Parents and children were scattered about, so whatever happened must've happened during the time school was letting out.

"What's going on?" Sosa asked, running up to a group of people standing at the gate.

Sosa pushed her way through the crowd and into the schoolyard where teachers and students had gathered. She was just about to run into the building, but then she saw Nyala standing with a group of kids next to her teacher.

"Mommy!" Nyala yelled, running up to Sosa.

"What's going on?" Sosa asked the teacher with a concerned look on her face.

"I'm not sure yet, but I think something happened to the Principal. I know when school let out cops just came from everywhere and wasn't allowing anybody to get back in the building," Nyala's teacher answered.

Sosa didn't need to hear anything else at that point.

Her child was safe and that was the most important thing at the moment. She was sure to catch everything else on the news, but in the meantime, getting Nyala home was her number one priority.

Basketball games were going down all day at the Rucker playground, and Qua and his lil' crew took up a whole section of the bleachers. Just about everybody that was somebody was out there shining and representing for their hoods. The basketball games were cool, but the main event was going down on the sidelines where some of the baddest bitches from all over NYC were being pressed upon by all the local getting-money players from around the city.

"Damn, what up Son?" Qua said, excited to see Ron after not hearing from him at all yesterday. "Pussy is cool my nigga but money is better," he joked.

Ron played unruffled and just laughed Qua off. "Yo, let me holla at you for a minute," Ron said, waving for Qua to take a walk with him.

Qua could tell from his tone that it must be something important. "Yeah, what up?" Qua said, walking next to Ron to the other side of the court.

"I'm at the spot right now putting the work together we just got from the chick and I was thinking we should make her our new line," Ron stated. "I didn't put it out on the streets yet, but when I cracked open a brick my mafuckin' nose hairs curled up," he joked.

Ron didn't know Sosa that well. The first time that he had met her was when Qua brought him to the coffee shop. He didn't even remember the name Qua asked for that day when they went there. All he knew was that they were able to buy 100 bricks of powder for the low-low prices. Ron figured that if he could sacrifice Sosa instead of Qua's original connect, he could stay out of jail and stay in the game at the same time.

"Let's see how this shit move first. Then I will see about hollering at Sosa to see if we can make this a permanent situation," Qua said, looking off at the game.

"Who da hell is Sosa?"

Qua looked at him like he was stupid. He'd been telling Ron who Sosa was since the first day they went to the shop. For him to forget that fast was crazy.

"Nigga you slippin,'" Qua commented with an irritating chuckle. Just let me handle everything. We gone be straight," he assured him.

"That's what's up. Let me get out of here and put this work together," Ron said, extending his hand to Qua before walking away.

"Alright, hit me up when you get done," Qua said, and turned away as if he was headed back to the game. But he actually waited and watched to see what car Ron came in. He found it a little odd that Ron had come down to the game only to inquire about changing the drug connect. What was even more alarming was that Ron parked way down the street, damn near a block away, when there was an open space right in front of the playground.

"Who da fuck wheels you got?" Qua mumbled, peeking his head out of the gate and seeing Ron pull off in a black Ford Taurus.

He only knew Ron to have a Maxima, which he used to transport cocaine throughout the city, and a Range Rover, which was his personal vehicle. Qua tried not to think anything of it, but his gut instinct was screaming something entirely differently. Qua made a mental note of it and decided to put a set of eyes on Ron to make sure he wasn't on no snitch shit.

"Yo kid," Qua called out to one of his youngins. "Yo, keep ya eyes out on that nigga Ron. He look a little stressed out or some shit," Qua told him, as he patted the young cat's back on their way back to the game.

It had only been a couple days but Sosa found herself right back in bed with Santos. Although she wasn't ready to admit it, he had become a source of comfort for her. When Sosa was with Santos she felt a sense of security that deep down she longed for.

"What's wrong wit' you? You haven't said a word in the last hour," Santos said, looking down at Sosa who was lying next to him in his bed. "And don't act like you asleep either," he joked, tickling the side of her neck to get her to move.

"Stop!" she giggled, smacking him on his bare chest. Ain't nothing wrong. I was just laying here thinking."

"Thinking about what?" Santos asked, trying to get

her to trust him enough to talk to him about the things that go in her life. Sosa had a few things on her mind, mainly pertaining to Semaj and what she was going through. She'd only been in the city for a minute and already she'd had to head back on account of some real, live drama.

"My life is so complicated, babe," Sosa began, scooting up a little closer to him. "I'm not who you think that I am."

"How about you give me a chance? I promise you can tell me anything and I am not gonna judge you or look at you any differently than I do now," Santos assured her.

Sosa lay there and thought about how badly she wanted to share her life with somebody else. No matter how hard of a role she had to portray in order to be a boss in the drug game, all she really wanted was to be somebody else's girl. She wanted to experience being in love with somebody, an emotion that she had never felt before for another man.

Sosa sat up in the bed, rolled over and straddled Santos so that she could look him in his eyes and say what was on her mind. Her naked body sitting on top of him was hard to resist. He reached up and tried to grab one of her breasts but Sosa playfully slapped his hand down before reaching over and pulling the sheet over her chest.

"Stop and listen to me," she smiled. "I heard everything you said to me last night about being in love with me. I swear, I wanna be able to say the same thing, but I don't think that I know how to love you. I mean, I've never been in love before. I don't know," Sosa exhaled, giving up on her choice of words.

Santos smiled and pulled her down to him so that her head rested on his chest. Just her trying to explain the way that she felt meant a lot to him. It made Santos want to protect her heart from ever being hurt. Not ever being in love was just as good as being a virgin in his eyes. Her heart was still pure and her feelings and emotions towards men had yet to develop, but Santos was there, willing and ready to be there for her.

"Let me teach you how to love," he spoke gently, stroking his fingers through her hair. "You just gotta trust me.

In that moment, Sosa felt safe. She felt like she could open up to him, and trust that he wouldn't hurt her. She felt like she could depend on him to be everything she needed in a man. She now wanted to share her world with him.

"I have to tell you something very important," she said, as she continued to lie on his chest.

"You can tell me anything," he reminded her, leaning down and kissing the top of her head.

It was a moment of silence in the room. It was so quiet all Sosa could hear was Santos' breathing.

"You ever heard of a person named Sosa?" she asked, then waited for a response.

"Yeah I heard he was a legend in the hood. People

say he still got the city on smash. Why, is that ya boyfriend or something?" Santos asked, pushing her chin up so that she was looking at him.

Sosa smiled, thinking about how people thought that she was a man. There were only a handful of people who knew who Sosa was; everybody else knew her as Samantha. She looked up at him and removed the smile from her face, not knowing how he was going to take it. It didn't matter, because it was time that he knew.

"I'm Sosa," she said, laying her head back on his chest.

Chapter 10

Two doctors, one nurse, and two armed guards stood outside of Vikingo's room preparing for the transport. Semaj sat in a chair next to his bed holding his hand. The doctor medically cleared Vikingo to be transferred via airplane to Manhattan Medical Center in New York. That was the only place Semaj could think of that could possibly save him. After seeing how they put Mitch back together after being shot multiple times there wasn't a doubt in her mind that the medical staff there would be able to help him.

"Señorita, the helicopter just landed on the roof," one of the doctors said, coming into the room.

Semaj got up, kissed Vikingo on his forehead and took one last look at him before the staff flooded the room. They unplugged this and that, lifted him onto a stretcher and wheeled him right out of the room.

"Round the clock watch," Semaj said, grabbing the arm of one of the guards she was sending with him. They went one way and Semaj went the other. She wasn't going to be making the trip to New York right now. She had other important things to take care of in Colombia and the first thing on her agenda was the local cartel. According to Gonzalez, the guerrillas that had taken over the warehouse were local. He knew that because of a tattoo that he'd seen on one of the gunmen.

The only problem was the fact that there were many, many drug cartels in Colombia. Three of them were local, all of which were extremely violent. But there was only one way to deal with the cartel, and that was to exterminate them altogether.

Sosa walked past the TV on her way into the kitchen to feed Nyala before she took her to school. Hearing the words "Little Rock," grabbed her attention, since that was the name of Nyala's school. She was shocked to hear the news anchor describe the brutal murder of the school Principal, and how no one was in custody for the murder as of yet.

"Get the hell out of here," Sosa said, taking a seat in front of the television to hear the rest.

"Here's a possible photo of the suspect police are looking for," the news anchor said as photos from the school's security camera popped up on the screen.

The pictures weren't that helpful, considering the large-framed glasses Paulette had on that covered almost half of her face. The footage showed her coming into the school, walking down the hallway and disappearing into the main office. However, the woman was never seen leaving the building.

"Little Rock will be closed today as the investigation of this murder continues," the news anchor said.

Sosa got up and headed back into the kitchen with Nyala, who was playfully eating her breakfast. "You wanna come to work with Mommy this morning?" Sosa leaned over and put her face up against the side of Nyala's.

Before Nyala could even answer her mother, the doorbell began to ring. Sosa waited for the nanny to answer the door and, when she did, Sosa could hear a man's voice identify himself as a detective. With caution, Sosa walked to the front of the house to see what was going on.

"Ms. Milano?" the detectives asked, seeing Sosa walking to the door. Only a few people knew Sosa's real name and where she really lived, so seeing the detective at her door was unusual. "I need to see some identification," Sosa stated, looking past the detectives to see what kind of vehicle they came in.

Both detectives quickly showed their badges and I.D. and Sosa checked them thoroughly. She was still kind of skeptical about letting them into her home, but the officers asked politely as though they had some imperative news.

"Ms. Milano, there was a murder at your daughter's school yesterday."

"I'm aware of that. I saw it on the news this morning. But why are you all here? You can't possibly be making a personal stop to every child's house that attends that school." Sosa asked, somewhat baffled.

Both detectives looked at each other for a second before one of them elected to speak. "The thing is, Ms. Milano, the suspect who we are looking for was trying to take your daughter out of school. She said that she was Nyala's aunt," the detective informed her.

Sosa felt a sharp pain in her chest that she was sure translated onto her face. She couldn't believe what she was hearing. Nyala didn't have any aunts around, especially one that would try to take her out of school without her permission, let alone kill the school Principal.

"What do you mean someone tried to take my daughter out of school? Nyala doesn't have any aunts in this city," Sosa retorted, as she felt her anger boiling to the point she was about to explode.

The detectives broke down all of the information the secretary had given them, including the Jamaican accent she had. When Sosa heard that, her Ox radar went up immediately. She had to think about that day when she put a bullet in between his eyes. For a second, she questioned whether or not he was dead. If anybody could survive a bullet to the head it would be Ox. He was like the devil in the flesh.

"Ms Milano, are you okay?" the detective asked, seeing that Sosa had drifted off.

"Yeah, I'm okay," Sosa lied, looking around the room in somewhat of a panic. "I'm going to have to ask you gentlemen to leave," she said, opening the door.

She had more than enough on her mind right now

and last thing she needed was to have a couple detectives up in her grill, drilling her. What if the person had been successful in doing what they set out to do and had walked out of the school with Nyala? Sosa would have been sick. Preventative measures needed to be taken immediately to ensure they wouldn't be successful the next time that they tried. Sosa wasn't going to waste any time in doing so.

"Nyala!" Sosa yelled as she looked out the window at the detectives pulling out of her driveway. "Hurry up with your breakfast. Today we're going on a trip," Sosa said, watching the street for any suspicious-looking cars.

Mitch sat in the diner reading the newspaper while he waited for his guests to join him. He glanced out the window and could see Qua pulling into the parking lot in a silver Benz. Both Qua and Ron got out of the car and Mitch could tell by the way they adjusted their clothes that both of them were strapped. This was a pre-scheduled meeting they had both decided to have when they ran into each other in the club.

There was a lot of bad blood between the two, but for some odd reason Qua wanted to put it all behind them. Mitch agreed in a sense, and decided to take Qua up on his offer to meet and talk. Of course, safety was of the utmost importance, so Mitch pulled the black .45 automatic from his shoulder strap and placed it on his lap. He kept a sharp eye on Ron as he stayed by the car while Qua came into the diner. Mitch waved his hand at

Qua, motioning for him to see where he was sitting.

"If it ain't Murda Mitch," Qua said with a devious grin on his face as he walked up to the table.

"What's good wit' you young blood?" Mitch said, folding the newspaper up and placing it over the gun on his lap.

Qua went right in. He wasn't the type to hold punches. When he had something on his mind, he said exactly how he felt. "You know, when I saw you the other night, I wanted to blow ya fuckin' head off," Qua began.

Here we go wit dis shit Mitch thought to himself. He slowly slid his hand under the newspaper after hearing that. "So why didn't you?" Mitch asked, wrapping his finger around the trigger.

"To be honest wit' you O.G…."

"You still love my daughter?" Mitch said, cutting Qua off and answering the question for him.

It was hard to explain the way he felt about Semaj but Mitch could see it in Qua's eyes. With everything they had been through and all of the females Qua had been with between the time of their separation and now, nobody could ever step foot in her shoes.

"I promised myself and Semaj that I would never hurt her again, even if that meant not being able to kill you," Qua divulged.

Mitch sat there and heard Qua out, and in a way he had a newfound respect for him. He didn't trust him as far as he could throw him, but he did respect how he felt.

"You know what, Qua, I hope that in the future we,"

he paused for a second to see who was calling. "Hold on, for a sec."

He was hesitant to take his hand off of his gun to see who it was. Qua just smiled. He knew from the moment he walked into the diner that Mitch had a gun pointed at him.

"It's cool O.G. I ain't here for dat," Qua chuckled.

Mitch smiled too, reaching into his pocket to grab his phone. "Speak of the devil," he said, answering the phone. "Hey Princess."

Semaj wasted no time telling Mitch everything that had went on with Vikingo, and how he was being transported to a hospital in New York. Qua sat, observing the concerned look on Mitch's face. It burned him up not to say something. He could even hear Semaj's voice slightly as she talked to her dad, and she sounded distraught.

"Alright, Princess. I'll check on him when he gets here," Mitch said, and then hung up.

It was quiet at the table for a second. Qua could tell that something was wrong. "Is she good?" Qua inquired, unable to conceal how worried he was.

Mitch didn't feel like getting into what was going on with Semaj, mainly because he didn't have all of the facts yet himself. "She's okay," he told Qua, then got back to the original conversation that they had been having.

Semaj stood in Valentina's room looking at herself in the large floor mirror. This room was off-limits for anybody to sleep in, but Semaj often came in there to clear her mind. The guerrillas had given her more than enough to think about. She knew that she had to respond with swiftness to the local cartel's thinking that she was weak.

"What should I do?" Semaj asked aloud as she stared at the large picture of Valentina hanging up on the wall. Semaj needed answers and she believed Valentina was the only person who could give them to her, even if she was dead.

"The cartels think that you are weak," a voice said.

Semaj thought that she was going crazy for a minute thinking Valentina was actually talking to her, that is, until she looked at the door and saw Maria standing there.

"You know if the cartel thinks that you are weak they will come after you. None of us will be safe," Maria cautioned, as she slowly entered the room. "I remember a time when the Medellín Cartel thought that she was weak," Maria said, looking up at the picture of Valentina on the wall. "She went into the city by herself and found the leader sitting in the coffee shop surrounded by five armed men."

Semaj looked on, intrigued by the story and wondering how it was going to end. "You could hear the sound of guns cocking the whole time as she walked towards him," Maria continued. "The cartel leader watched as she slowly approached, waving for his men to lower their weapons. I don't know if he thought that Valentina was coming there to talk, or maybe he really did think that she was weak."

"What did she do?" Semaj asked, wanting Maria to finish. "Tell me Maria," she said.

"She pulled a large revolver from her waist, cocked the hammer back and pointed it directly at his head. His guards raised their guns and pointed them at Valentina. The leader went to utter some words but never got the chance. With no fear, no hesitation, no remorse or any indication that she was afraid to die, Valentina pulled the trigger, sending a bullet to the center of his head."

"Damn, Valentina," Semaj said, thinking about how vicious her grandmother was.

"The guards never fired a single shot at her," Maria continued with a smile on her face. "Vikingo said he and the rest of the guards didn't shoot her because they all felt she displayed the actions of a warrior. That was the cartel Vikingo was with before he vowed his loyalty to the Espreilla Family."

Semaj looked back up at the picture of her grandmother. She didn't know how a woman could be so brave and go so hard, even in the storm of defeat. The words from the guerrilla telling Semaj that she was no Valentina had resonated with her. It had Semaj doubting herself. She questioned if she was cut out to run the most powerful cartel in Colombia.

"It's time for you to step up and become a warrior, Semaj," Maria stated, taking Semaj's hand into hers. "Our family depends on it," she said, kissing her hand and then walking out of the room.

It was at that very instant Semaj knew what needed

to be done. Something Maria had said made Semaj grasp that her purpose in life was bigger than selling drugs. She had a name to honor and that name was Espreilla. Along with that, she had a family to protect, and Semaj was willing to do that at all costs.

"I'ma hold you down, Grandma," Semaj stated confidently, walking over and grabbing her Glock off of the table before heading out of the room.

Sosa sat at the window looking up and down the street for any suspicious movement. She was on high alert and had been for the past few hours after the detectives left. Her mind was consumed by what they had said and she kept replaying it over and over again in her head. That, along with the surveillance photos the news posted this morning, made Sosa ultimately arrive at the conclusion that it would be safer to get Nyala out of the country. Getting her out of the city wasn't going to be enough, because if in fact it was Ox and his people coming to take Nyala back, Sosa knew they would be relentless in their pursuit. That's the reason why two fully-loaded .45 automatics sat on Sosa's lap as she continued to gaze out the window.

"Mommy! Mommy!" Nyala yelled, coming down the steps. "I packed my Princess dress," she giggled, swaying side to side.

"You did?" Sosa smiled, playfully pinching her belly. Ms. Edna came down the steps with a tiresome look on her face. She could barely carry the two large suitcases she had in her hands. "You sure you got everything?" Sosa asked in amusement.

"This little girl wouldn't leave without half of this stuff," Edna joked, walking over and sitting the suitcases by the door. "She acted like she wasn't coming back."

Sosa looked around the house and honestly didn't know if Nyala ever would come back. Dealing with those crazy Jamaicans meant anything was possible; Sosa needed to take at least three steps for every one they made. Sosa's own safety wasn't the issue, it was Nyala's. If they had to relocate permanently to guarantee her daughter's safety, Sosa was willing to do so.

She got up and walked over to grab her cell phone that was sitting by the TV, then took a seat on the couch. She had to make a couple quick phone calls to get a few things taken care of before she left. As Sosa put the phone up to her ear, Nyala walked over and sat in between her legs.

"What's up, Penny?" Sosa said, grabbing a handful of Nyala's hair and putting it into a ponytail. "I gotta go outta town for a couple of days and I need you to take care of something for me."

Chapter 11

Whatever cartel had stormed her land had also given Semaj 24 hours to leave Colombia. Within that time, she had put together a small army and set out for the city of Corinto. That is where Hector Torez ran the Couca Cartel. He owned a couple hundred acres of coca fields and produced a significant amount of cocaine on a weekly basis, which was sold mainly in Mexico.

Semaj drove into the marketplace where Torez's headquarters were. She was accompanied by five armored black-on-black Suburbans. Heads turned as they sped down the road kicking up dust.

"Everybody in this truck comes with me. Make sure everybody else secures the perimeter," Semaj instructed, cocking her Glock back slightly to make sure that she had a bullet in the chamber.

Semaj's truck came to a stop in front of the lumber building that was used as a front for Torez's business. Two trucks sped around and got in front of her while three trucks pulled up behind her. Semaj's men jumped out of the trucks and proceeded to the building like

SWAT. Torez's men wasted no time opening fire from the rooftop of the lumber building and from buildings across the street.

"Senor, la policia esta aqui," Torez's lieutenant said coming into the office.

Torez could hear the gun battle ensuing outside. He jumped up out of his chair and looked out the window to get a better look at what was going on outside. His lieutenant said that the police were there, but Torez didn't recognize the men.

"It's not the cops," Torez said, walking over to his cabinet and grabbed a 203 rifle with a grenade launcher on it. He and his lieutenant headed out of the office, guns hot. They could hear the gunfire getting louder and louder as they approached the steps that led to the first floor.

"Stay here Señorita," Gonzalaz instructed Semaj as his team ran through the whole first floor.

Torez's men were making a stand though. They were coming from everywhere, gunning down Semaj's men. Semaj was literally ducking and dodging bullets left and right. The sounds of men screaming at each other in Spanish along with guns blazing filled the air.

"Dejar de disparar! Dejar de disparar!," Torez yelled, telling his men to stop shooting.

Semaj waved at her men to do the same. The gunfire outside continued, however. Except for the sounds of clips dropping and guns cocking, it was silent on the first level.

"Do you know who you're fucking with?" Torez belted from the top of the stairway. "This is Couca!" he yelled, repping the name of his cartel.

Semaj got up from behind the concrete partition that separated the room she was in from the room Torez and his men were in. Gonzalez went to grab her before she walked into the firing zone but Semaj stopped him. "Oye Hector!" she yelled out, slowly walking towards the other room.

Hearing his name, Hector cautiously made his way down the steps. His men formed somewhat of a barrier at the bottom of the steps for him as a means to protect him. "All I want is you. You can save the lives of your men if you just sacrifice yours," Semaj said, partially stepping into the open room.

"Save my men? Look around, Señorita, my men are ready and willing to die for me," Hector shot back. "If you turn around and leave, I'll think about letting you leave my city in one piece," he threatened.

"I can't do that Hector. You already gave me 24 hours to leave my land and that is going to cost you your life," Semaj said, thinking that he was the one behind the guerrilla attack.

Torez looked at his lieutenant with a confused look on his face. He didn't know what Semaj was talking about. He was still unaware of who she was, for that matter. "I don't know where you get your information from but got the wrong man. I didn't give you 24 hours to leave."

"You sent guerrillas to my fields yesterday."

"I didn't send no one," Hector screamed back in frustration, cutting her off and pushing his way to the front.

Semaj looked over at Gonzalez who shook his head, indicating Torez wasn't the one who sent the guerillas. If he had, he would have already owned up to it and the gun battle would have continued. Had he denied it, and really had sent the guerillas after her, his men would have looked at him like he was weak for not owning up to it. Semaj had hit a dead end in trying to find out who it was that wanted her gone.

All wasn't lost, though. She had come too far to turn back, and in all honesty, she really didn't want to. She had to establish dominance in Colombia in order to keep the family name strong. Semaj looked at Hector and then back over at Gonzalez. In an instant, she leveled her gun and began firing in Torez's direction, striking him once in the chest before his guards were able to pull him behind them. They didn't hesitate in the least in opening fire on Semaj who ran sideways, firing into the crowd of gunmen before diving behind the partition with Gonzalez. Gonzalez shook his head and smiled at Semaj's bravery. He then called for back-up from his men outside, who by this time had secured the outer perimeter. They rushed in like a tactical unit, killing everything in a matter of seconds and leaving nothing but gun smoke in the air and debris scattered about.

Vikingo survived the flight from Colombia to New York but his condition had gotten worse. He still had internal bleeding, and now he was having trouble breathing. Time was of the essence. When MedEvac landed the helicopter on the roof of Manhattan Medical, Mitch was standing right there with a medical team waiting for him too. Vikingo was prepped and ready for surgery within minutes of being at the hospital.

Sosa was driving down the highway on her way to JFK when her phone began to ring. She reached down, grabbed the phone from the center console and saw that it was Penny calling. Sosa instantly remembered the new shipment of cocaine that was due to come through today.

"I know, I know," Sosa said, answering the phone. She had been so caught up with the attempted abduction situation that she'd pretty much forgotten about everything else.

"We got a little problem with the shipment again," Penny said, sitting at a table outside of a coffee shop.

Sosa rolled her eyes in frustration. She really couldn't afford to miss another delivery. Shit was getting kind of tight and Qua had put a real dent in her supplies when he bought 100 kilos.

"Are they late again? Cause if they're late..."

"No, it's not that. The problem is that there's two

cops sitting in an unmarked car a block away and they're eyeing this spot," Penny said, as she discretely looked down the street in their direction.

"Are you sure they're watching us?" Sosa asked, looking in her rearview mirrors for any unwanted tailing.

"Not 100% sure, but I really don't wanna take any chances with making the drop here at the coffee shop," Penny said, as she watched pedestrians pass by.

Sosa thought about it for a second. The risk was high but the product was needed. Going through with the delivery would go against everything she knew, but times were getting hard. "Look, when they get there, re-direct them to the other drop location in Brooklyn," Sosa said, referring to her club. "If shit still looks funny then you know what to do," Sosa instructed, before hanging up the phone.

She pulled into JFK, still checking her rearview for anything suspicious. Ever since the incident with Ox, Jamaicans had Sosa paranoid. All she wanted to do was get Nyala somewhere safe until she had a chance to deal with the situation herself. Whoever was looking for Nyala would eventually strike again, and when they did, Sosa was going to be waiting for them.

"Señorita, everyone back at the compound is safe, Gonzalez informed Semaj as they drove out of Corinto.

Semaj looked out of the window in a daze. This was the first time she'd ever conquered somebody else's land and she had to admit it was exciting. Semaj could see why Valentina was addicted to the power that she had possessed in Colombia.

"So what do you wanna do with the land?" Semaj was so completely caught up in her own thoughts that at first she didn't hear Gonzalez call her name. "Semaj!" Gonzalez yelled again, this time snapping her out of her daze.

"Huh?" she replied turning her face towards him.

"What do you wanna do with the land?" he asked, as he continued to drive.

Semaj thought about it. For her it wasn't even about the coca fields or the money she could have possibly made from taking over the cartel. Something more important was riding on the table and Semaj realized it now more than ever. It had to be known that she was not that Bitch to be fucked with in Colombia, because if you did, you were playing with your livelihood.

"Burn the coco field and then give the land back to the honest people of the city," Semaj said, turning back to stare out the window.

Chapter 12

Paulette entered the coffee shop a little after twelve in the afternoon. There weren't that many customers, but any minute now the lunch crowd would pack Sosa's place. Penny stood behind the bar filling up the espresso machine, unaware of who'd just walked in. She picked her head up from the machine to see Paulette's reflection in the mirror.

"Oh, I'm sorry, can I get you anything?" Penny asked, wiping her hands off with a towel.

"I'm looking for Sosa," Paulette said, looking around the coffee shop. "Is she here?" she asked, taking a good look at her surroundings.

"I'm sorry. Who are you again?" Penny shot back with one eyebrow raised, detecting the Jamaican accent.

There were only a handful of people in the city who knew Sosa by that name, and Penny knew just about all of them. She definitely wasn't aware of any Jamaicans that Sosa dealt with on a first-name basis.

"Is she 'er? Me won talk to 'er," Paulette said, getting a little fidgety.

Penny noticed the bulge in Paulette's waist and the way she looked around the shop as if she was checking to see if anybody was watching her. It made Penny nervous, and the closest gun she could get to was at the other end of the bar under the register. Fear of being shot in her back is what made Penny think before she moved.

"She's not here but I can give her a call if it's something important," Penny responded. "I just gotta get her number from the back," she said, walking off towards the office.

Penny could see the butt of the gun under the cash register and the closer she got to it, the safer she felt. She didn't even look back to see where Paulette was, and by the time she walked up on the register, grabbed the 9mm and spun around, Paulette had vanished. Penny's heart was racing. She didn't know how that situation was going to play out and the one thing she couldn't afford right now was the cops running up in the shop. Not only would the shooting draw a lot of attention to the shop, the 100 kilos of pure cocaine in the basement would surely have Penny booked up to the moon.

Semaj and Sosa sat on the bench looking out at Nyala playing with the other kids in the swimming pool. Nyala loved coming to Colombia to stay with Aunt Semaj. It was like her second home and all the kids loved her. That's the reason why Sosa brought her there.

"Are you sure that's Ox's people?" Semaj asked, still

a little shocked that someone would try and take Nyala from school.

"Yeah, I just don't know who it is. I saw the pictures on the news but I didn't recognize the chick."

"Señorita," Gonzalez interrupted. "Can I have a word with you?"

Semaj got up from the bench and joined him off to the side. Sosa continued watching the kids play but periodically looked over at the two of them conversing. Within a couple of minutes Semaj walked back over to Sosa.

"I need you to hear this," Semaj said, motioning for Sosa to follow her.

Gonzalez led them to the front gates of the compound where Raphael Lopez stood with his entourage. Raphael was the leader of the San Pedro Cartel and was probably the third most feared man in Colombia. He was also the head of the next cartel on Semaj's list to conquer, so it surprised her to see him standing in front of her home.

"To what do I owe the pleasure?" Semaj said, walking up to the front gates with Sosa right beside her.

"I don't remember Valentina ever being so unwelcoming," Raphael said, grabbing the tall gates that separated them from each other.

Semaj nodded her head at one of her men to open up the gates, seeing that Raphael came with a more humble approach than anything. He entered, but stopped his men from coming inside so that there wouldn't be any tension in the air.

"So why are you here?" Semaj asked, slowly walking alongside of Raphael as she led him into the compound. He noticed that Sosa was walking along with them and hesitated to talk. Semaj noticed his concern. "It's okay. Whatever you have to say to me, she can hear it," she conveyed to Raphael.

He smiled at her, but not for that reason. Semaj reminded him of Valentina so much. It was rumored that he and her had a thing for each other back in the day, but nobody knew to what extent.

"I am here out of respect for your grandmother first and foremost. She was a very powerful woman Semaj, so know that filling her shoes won't be easy. Semaj listened on. "Now, I am here for a couple of reasons and I guess I should start with this ... If you think that you can take over my cartel like you did Hector's, you are sadly mistaken. I have a great deal of respect for your organization, but I promise you, you will lose going up against me," Raphael said, stopping in his tracks to give Semaj a stern look.

Semaj nodded her head with a smile. She respected him for that. It didn't mean that she wouldn't kill him right where he stood, because she would, but all that depended on what came out of his mouth next. "The other reason why I'm here is to inform you that it's someone from the 16 tent who wants you dead. This is a fact. I got word from a highly trusted associate," Raphael said.

"What do you mean someone from the 16 Tent?"

Semaj asked, completely caught off guard by that disclosure.

Raphael didn't know all of the facts to the plot but what he did know was enough. He explained to Semaj that a group of soldiers from the Valle Cartel were overheard by one of his people in a bar, arguing about who from the 16 Tent was going to pay them after the job was done. He couldn't give Semaj a name because the soldiers never said one but his people were positive they heard 16 Tent being mentioned.

"And why are you telling me this again?" Semaj inquired, waiting to hear a catch behind it.

"Like I said before. Your grandmother was a dear friend of mine and if it was her that was standing where you are, I would have told her too," Raphael said, "So this bloodshed you're causing is against the wrong people. We're not the enemies, someone from the 16 Tent is." With that said, Raphael walked back towards the front gates.

He left both Semaj and Sosa speechless as they stood there and watched Raphael leave the compound. The 16 Tent meeting in New York was two days away and Semaj didn't have the slightest idea of who would want her dead. All business and friendships up until now had been on the up and up, and everybody seemed to be happy. It was mind-boggling that a member of what was supposed to be like an extended family would cross her. But before Semaj appeared at the 16 Tent meeting, she was going to find out who betrayed her. The only way she was going to get that information was by applying a little more pressure in the right spot.

Semaj looked at Sosa and Sosa looked back at her. She didn't even have to say the words because Sosa already knew what was up. She wanted to know just as bad as Semaj did who it was that wanted her dead. "Gonzalez!" Semaj yelled, waving him over to her.

"Yes, Senorita," he said, coming right over.

"Bump up the security on the compound. I need a team of five cars to come with me," she instructed while walking into the house.

"Where are we going, if I may ask?" Gonzalez asked, so he would know which men he should bring. Semaj stopped, turned and faced him. She had nothing but fury in her eyes and was set on her target.

"We're going into the jungle," she said, and then turned and walked off.

Edna did everything that Sosa instructed her do as far as getting rid of everything in Nyala's room. In the event the Jamaicans found out where she lived, Sosa didn't want there to be any signs of a child living there. She hoped that it would deter them from looking for Nyala there again.

Edna was taking the last of Nyala's things out to the car when she first noticed the car parked at the end of the driveway. It was nighttime, but Edna could tell that somebody was in the car due to the light smoke that was coming from the exhaust pipe. Even still, she continued to load the last of Nyala's toys that were in the storage bin into the backseat of her car, all the while keeping an eye on the suspicious vehicle. She kind of rushed so that she could get back into the house to call the cops and report it.

Edna turned around and was heading back into the house when she stopped dead in her tracks seeing a man on the steps. She looked back at the suspicious car knowing that she hadn't noticed anybody getting out of it. She turned back towards the man, scared to death to even move.

"Come on. I am not gonna hurt you," Patrick said, taking a puff of the spliff he had in his hand.

Edna was about to turn on her heels and make a break for it once she heard the Jamaican accent, but right before she did the sound of a car door slamming broke her train of thought. She went to look back at the suspicious car and saw that a female had exited and now had a gun in her hand.

"We just gotta ask you a few questions," Patrick said, waving for Edna to come up the steps.

She really didn't have a choice because Paulette was about five feet away from her with the gun pointed in her direction. She looked around, hoping for any of the neighbors to come out of their houses and see what was going on. There was nobody there to help her; the only thing she could do was comply and hope that they wouldn't kill her.

"Move!" Paulette said, pushing the gun into her back as they walked up the steps.

Qua could smell the rain in the air the moment he rolled his window down. Ron jumped out of his black Range Rover Sport and slowly maneuvered his way through the traffic to cross Canal Street. "Did you see where he went?" Qua asked Ron when he walked up to his car.

"Yeah, he went into the hospital for something," Ron said, keeping a watchful eye on the cars that kept shooting past him. "I think he's on the 6th floor though. When he got on the elevator by himself, it stopped on the 6th floor," Ron confirmed.

From the moment Qua and Mitch parted ways at the diner, Qua had him followed. He was more concerned about Semaj than anything and he could tell by the intense conversation Mitch and Semaj had over the phone that something was wrong. Once he got confirmation, Qua wanted to be the first person to be there for her.

"Alright homie, that's good lookin'," Qua said, extending his hand out the window for a dap. "Oh, and how's that other thing moving?" he said, referring to the cocaine he got off of Sosa.

"I'ma keep it 100 wit' you. We need to be buying our shit from Shorty, son. Our people lovin' that shit," Ron said, sticking his hand into the car for another dap.

Sosa's cocaine was pure, raw, and uncut. One could easily turn one kilo into two kilos if that person knew what he was doing. "Cool. I'ma get up with you," Qua said, rolling up his window.

He watched Ron zigzag his way across the street, and once he got to his car safely Qua pulled off into traffic.

Patrick punched Edna in her face for the tenth time, knocking blood out of her mouth. She sat in the chair in the middle of the living room with her hands tied behind the chair. She'd been beaten for over 30 minutes and she still hadn't spoken a word. That's what made Patrick and Paulette even more irritated.

"Tell us where Sosa and Nyala is and all of this will stop," Paulette said, lifting Edna's face up to look at her.

Edna rolled her eyes and snatched her chin out of Paulette's hand. She still wasn't saying a word. Her loyalty to Sosa and Nyala ran deeper than any pain either one of them could inflict on her. She had already walked into the house with the intentions of dying.

"Look at me....Hey, look at me," Paulette said, tapping the side of Edna's head with her gun. Edna cut her only good eye over at her. "All I want is me niece. Sosa stole her from us and all we want to do is take her home," Paulette said, trying to use the sympathy card.

Paulette's words were dead to Edna as soon as they left her poisonous mouth. At this point, all she was hoping was for her death to happen sooner rather than later so her suffering would cease. Patrick walked up beside Edna, took another pull of weed and then pushed the burning tip of the spliff into her good eye. She screamed at the top of her lungs in agony as she rolled out of the chair onto the floor. Patrick grabbed a handful of her hair and lifted her back up into the chair.

"Tell us where she's at," Paulette yelled, hoping that made her change her mind. It didn't. Edna's cries actually started to turn into laughter as a way to mock them. Paulette was tired of the games. She came to the conclusion that Edna wasn't going to talk.

She put the 9mm up to Edna's head and right before she pulled the trigger, a phone started ringing in the house. Patrick and Paulette looked around to see where the ringing sound was coming from. Paulette quickly spotted the phone on the charger sitting inside the entertainment system.

"Right there," she snapped, pointing so Patrick could grab it.

She took the phone from him, looked at the screen and saw a cell phone number with the letter S in front of it. She knew that it had to be Sosa. "Hello Sosa," Paulette answered, walking slowly towards the front of the house away from Patrick and Edna.

Sosa's heart dropped into her stomach at the sound of the Jamaican accent. The first person that she thought of was Edna. If they had answered her phone, she was either dead or about to be dead.

"You're not gonna get her," Sosa responded as she sat there and watched Nyala finally fall asleep in her bed.

"See, dats where you wrong. She might be ya child but she has my brother's blood running through her veins."

Sosa got up from the chair that she was sitting in and walked into the bathroom. Her mind raced as she thought about Ox's siblings and which one could be capable of going through all this trouble for Nyala. Most of his family wasn't into the street life, but there was one person that Sosa knew was certifiably bat-shit crazy. If it was who she thought it was, Sosa knew that she was gonna have her hands full.

"Paulette?" Sosa asked, staring into the phone like she could see her.

Paulette smiled. "Yeaaaaa mon. And since you know that's it's me looking for you now, you better vanish off the face of this earth, because that's the only way me not gone find you," Paulette threatened as she peeked out the window to make sure Edna's screams didn't attract neighbors.

"Well, you ain't gotta worry about coming to find me. I'll be to see you very, very soon," Sosa replied.

"Let me give you something to think about until then," Paulette said, walking across the room to Edna. "Say goodbye to your friend."

Pop! Pop! Pop! Paulette shot Edna three times, all in her chest, knocking her out of the chair. Sosa had to take the phone away from her ear. She hung up. She knew that Paulette had just killed Edna and to hear it for herself was a tough blow. She put her back up against the wall and slid down until she was sitting on the floor. She was going to take this time to do all her grieving for Edna now because the problems she had on her plate weren't going to allow her to grieve later.

Raul walked up and took a seat at the bar next to Nikolai. He pulled his phone from his back pocket, looked at it and then placed it on the bar in front of him. Nikolai was the one who wanted to meet with Raul to discuss the details of his assassination against Semaj. She didn't want anything to go wrong because all it took was for him to make one mistake and both of them were up the river without a paddle.

"I see Marco's not too enthused about the whole situation," Raul began as he motioned for the bartender to come over and serve him. "Are you sure we can trust that he won't say anything?"

Nikolai waited for the bartender to leave before she responded to Raul's comment. "I will have what he's having," Raul told the bartender.

"Marco's backing out. He really doesn't want to be involved with it, but he did give me his word that he would never speak of it to anybody," Nikolai said, lifting the shot glass up to her mouth.

They both sat there in silence as the bartender walked back over with Raul's drink. It didn't take but a second for him to drop the drink off, because he could feel that his presence was unwanted.

"Do you need any help with this?" Nikolai asked Raul after the bartender left.

"No, my people in Colombia are taking care of everything as we speak. My men are good at what they do."

"Good, because Semaj has to go. Her family is taking over the whole damn Tent," Nikolai spat, before downing the rest of her drink. "The longer she stays alive, the more all of our seats are in jeopardy," she complained, and then got up, tossed a fifty-dollar bill on the bar for her drink, and walked off.

Raul sat there taking his time sipping his drink slowly. He pondered what Nikolai had said about Semaj's family taking over the Tent. He'd never looked at it that way, and now he knew Nikolai's true motivation behind wanting to get Semaj out of the way. Raul dug into his pocket, pulled out some money and placed it on the bar, then grabbed his cell phone and looked at it again before putting it back in his pocket. Nikolai had no idea she'd just given him another insurance policy, a policy he would perhaps have to cash in on in the future.

Ron stopped at the light on 118th and Broadway, reached into the center console and grabbed his cell phone. When he lifted his head back up he noticed a black Crown Victoria pulling right up next to his ride. He rolled his eyes in frustration, knowing exactly who it was. The dark tinted window on the passenger side rolled down and out popped Agent Mason's head.

"Follow us," he instructed, before rolling his window back up.

Ron did what he was told, pulling off behind them. He followed them to a dark side street where Mason and Agent Davis pulled over and parked in a vacant lot. Ron looked around before pulling into the lot, thinking to himself how this would be the perfect location to kill somebody. He actually had visions of emptying out his whole clip at Mason and Davis, but came back to his senses once he pulled into the parking space next to their car.

"Tell me something good before I put you in jail right now," Agent Davis yelled, from the driver side as Ron rolled his window down.

"I told you that I got you," Ron responded in a frustrated voice.

"That's not good enough. I let you ride for a couple of days now and you still ain't brought me shit," Agent Davis barked, as he rolled down the back, passenger side window. "Don't get it fucked up. I can make this shit reappear just as fast as I made it disappear," he threatened.

Ron looked in the backseat of the Crown Victoria and could see three bricks of cocaine and the gun they took from his car. "These mafuckas is vicious," Ron thought to himself.

Davis wanted to remind Ron that he still had the evidence and he could book him at anytime. With that looming over his head, he would never be free until he did what the agents wanted.

"Look, I need a couple more days to get rid of the coke I got left. Me and my man got a new connect named Sosa. He supposed to be getting a lot of work in. That's all I know right now," Ron said.

When they heard the name Sosa, Agent Davis and Mason looked at each other. This was the first time they heard somebody use that name since Javier told them that he was delivering the cocaine to somebody named Sosa at the coffee shop.

"What you know about Sosa?" Davis probed, damn near breaking his neck to look out the window.

"I don't know shit about the nigga yet. As soon as you let me get back to doin' what I was doin' I can get you more information," Ron answered in an irritated tone.

He really didn't like that he had become an informant for the feds. A rat was the last thing he had ever imagined that he would be. It was eating at him, but Agent Davis didn't care two shits about how he felt, nor did he mind Ron selling the rest of the coke he had so that he could get the information that he needed. Davis's new mission in life was to bring Sosa down at all costs, and whoever else was associated with her organization. But first, he had to find out who and where Sosa was, and the only way he could do that right now was by giving Ron a couple more days.

"Have something for me very soon or start looking for a lawyer," Davis threatened before backing out of the lot.

Chapter 13

Back to back, Semaj and her men sped down the narrow, wet, rocky road that led them into the jungle where the Valle Cartel operated. They were one of the more ruthless cartels in Colombia and their knowledge of the jungle was impeccable, unlike Semaj, who had never been into the jungle until today.

"What's wrong?" Semaj asked Sosa, seeing that she was in a trance. "You haven't said but two words this morning."

Sosa was thinking about Edna and how she had been murdered in cold blood trying to protect Nyala. She knew that Paulette was like the devil and that her madness wasn't going to stop there.

"That problem back home is getting worse," Sosa answered, not really wanting to talk about it.

"Well, we can go deal with it."

"Señorita! We are about to cross into their territory," Gonzalez told Semaj as he pointed out symbols that were carved into a couple of the trees they passed by.

Semaj looked out the window and saw nothing but

trees and bushes everywhere. This was the first time that she'd been in a real live jungle. Sosa was captivated as well, as this was also her first time.

"Yo, this is crazy," Sosa said as she gazed out the window.

The truck rocked from side to side as it plowed through the muddy road. Semaj rolled her window down and could hear all kinds of birds chirping in the trees, but within a couple of minutes of riding along, the scenery began to change. Sosa looked up one of the trees and swore that she saw somebody sitting in it. She turned to look at Semaj who was also looking up into the trees.

"Did you see that?" Sosa asked, making sure her eyes weren't playing tricks on her as she looked back out of her window.

The Valle Cartel had over 300 field workers along with 150-armed guards that secured 700 acres of coca fields. They had men on the ground and men in the trees along with men by the riverbanks. Their tactics in dealing with intruders were different. The heavily armed men didn't stop you from coming into their territory; coming in was exactly what they wanted. It was being able to leave the jungle alive that was the real test.

"We have company," the head of security announced, coming into the tent. Ricardo Gomez lifted his head to look at the many monitors he had off to the side. Gomez was the leader of the Valle Cartel and ran his organization with an iron fist. The one thing that he didn't appreciate was people showing up on his land uninvited. "You want us to stop them at the leverage point?" the guard asked, looking at the monitors behind him. Gomez watched as Semaj and her five vehicles drove down the narrow road. He could tell that the vehicles were armored and probably could withstand a lot of gunfire. Whoever was inside was of importance, and that piqued Gomez's curiosity.

"No, don't stop them. Let them come to me," Gomez stated, staring into the monitor.

Something ain't right," Sosa said, tapping Semaj's leg.

She could feel it and Gonzalez could feel it too. He was expecting to have been fired upon by now, or at least confronted by the cartel's guerrillas. Every armed man they passed just let them go deeper and deeper into the jungle.

"Up ahead," Gonzalez said, pointing in front of him. "Look alive," he notified his men through the walkie-talkies to let them know to stay on point.

There was a small camp consisting of one large tent and several other smaller tents surrounding it. Semaj's men fanned out in the trucks when one of the narrow roads became spacious enough. Two out of the five trucks fell back. Semaj's truck and another truck pulled right up in front of the large tent, where everybody exited with guns locked and loaded, except for Semaj and Sosa, who stayed inside.

A moment of silence took over the jungle. Even the birds stopped chirping. All of a sudden, men armed with AK-47s rushed out from everywhere yelling and screaming. They came from out of the tents, jumped out of the trees and dashed out of the bush.

"Prepararse para la guerra se preparan para la guerra!" several of the guerrillas yelled, pointing their guns at Semaj and her people.

Gonzalez and his team weren't backing down. They kept their guns pointed right back at them, yelling and screaming for them to do the same. Semaj may have looked outnumbered, but what she lacked in manpower she made up for with skills. Every last one of her men were sharpshooters and from the way they had positioned themselves around the armored trucks, they were going to do a lot of damage in a very short period of time.

All of the guerrillas got quiet once Gomez walked out from under the tent. Semaj saw him and got out of the truck with Sosa on her heels. Gomez knew off the bat Semaj had to be the boss because of the way she dressed. She was dripped in power red from her pantsuit all the way to her five-inch heel shoes.

"What's your business here?" Gomez asked, standing in between two of his men.

"I heard you gave me 24 hours to leave my land. I thought that I would come see you in person so that we can discuss your ultimatum," Semaj said, standing in between two of her own men.

Now Gomez knew exactly who she was. He was surprised that she had come all this way to talk. Little did he know Semaj had another agenda. He looked at her and then at her men, then yelled for his men to lower their weapons. He waved for Semaj to come into the tent. Gonzalez and a few of his men along with Sosa walked behind her, but Gomez stopped them and told Semaj that she could only bring two people inside with her. Gonzalez and Sosa entered with her while the rest of her men stayed outside.

Gomez took a seat at his desk. His men stood off to the side while Semaj, Sosa and Gonzalez stood in front of his desk. It was quiet for a moment. "You here to talk, so talk," Gomez said, sitting back down in his chair arrogantly.

"You know that I'm not going to just leave my land," Semaj said, taking a seat in the chair in front of his desk. "And to be honest with you, I think you have bitten off more than you can chew. You and I both know that I could have one thousand men tearing this jungle apart within the hour," she said, kicking her feet up on his table. "But I think we can come to some sort of mutual understanding if you simply tell me who put you up to this."

Sosa could see what direction Semaj was going with the conversation. She wanted to find out which member from the 16 Tent wanted her dead. Just flat out killing Gomez wasn't going to help her get the answers she was looking for, so a different approach had to be taken.

"Ahhh! You wanna know who's betraying you," Gomez said in a mischievous voice. "Now that's going to cost you," he said, crossing his hands over his stomach.

"What do you want?" Semaj pried, taking her feet off the table and sitting straight up in the chair.

"I want half of your coca field."

"How 'bout I sweeten the deal and make you an even better offer?"

"Really? Let me find out that you're very generous. Please tell me what else you are offering." Gomez questioned, as his eyes began to sparkle in anticipation of what else Semaj could proposing.

"Gomez, you caught me on an excellent day," Semaj smiled, showcasing her perfect pearly whites. "I am in a very generous mood. So after you tell me who betrayed me, not only will I thank you for the information but I'll also let you live. See how considerate I am?" Semaj gave a slight smirk and leaned comfortably in the chair before kicking her feet back up on the table.

"Let me live? The audacity of you!" Gomez bawled, full of anger and resentment in his voice. "The only reason why you're still alive is because I let you live. My men will destroy you!" he continued to yell, pounding his fist down on the table.

"Tell me who it is." Unlike Gomez, Semaj spoke calmly, not even breaking a slight sweat. She rose to her feet, showing no signs of fear.

Everybody in the room tensed up. Gonzalez

gripped his AR-15 tighter as he scanned his surroundings. The two men with Gomez also had their fingers on the triggers. Sosa had already taken the safety off the 5.7 she had in her hand.

"You wanna know who it is?" You wanna know who it is?" Gomez repeated, with his voice rising as he pulled on a .357 revolver from his gun holster that was wrapped around his waist.

He was hyper and had a crazed look in his eyes. He popped the barrel out, emptied all the bullets but two, spun it twice, and then snapped the barrel back into the gun. "You wanna play a game? Let's play a game," Gomez said, slamming the gun on the table.

Semaj glared at him like he was a straight fool, but he was dead-ass serious.

"You ever heard of Russian Roulette?" Gomez asked.

"You must have bumped ya mutha fuckin' head," Sosa cut in, raising the 5.7 pistol and pointing it at Gomez.

"Baja el arma ahora!" Gomez's men yelled pointing their guns at her.

"Fuck you," Sosa replied, disregarding their demands.

"Wait a minute! Wait a minute!" Semaj yelled, trying to calm everybody down. "You wanna play, let's play," Semaj said, leaning on the table.

Gomez waved for his men to lower their guns, which they did, and then he pushed the revolver across the table to Semaj. "There's two bullets in the gun on opposite sides of the barrel. If you manage not to blow your head off four times I'll tell you everything you want to know, but if your brains go flying across the room, I get to have your land," Gomez said, with a serious look on his face.

"And what about you?" Semaj asked.

"Oh, me?" I don't play. It's just you," Gomez answered.

"You fuckin' lunatic. Don't do that shit Maj," Sosa argued.

Semaj looked down at the gun and then back at Gomez. Before Sosa could say another word, Semaj picked up the gun, cocked the hammer back, pressed it to her temple and pulled the trigger.

Click! Sosa had turned her head when Semaj pulled the trigger thinking that it was over for her.

Semaj popped the barrel out, spun it, then slapped it back into the gun. She didn't hesitate for one second putting the gun to her head and pulling the trigger. Click! She didn't blink or budge, nor did she take her eyes off of Gomez while she was doing it.

"Come on Maj, that's enough," Sosa said, walking up next to her. "We'll find another way."

Semaj was determined to find out what she wanted to know. She felt as though without the information, she was as good as dead anyway. If a member from the 16 Tent wanted you dead, 9 times out of 10 you were going to be killed. Semaj took the barrel out, spun it again, then slapped it back into the gun. Sosa just backed off and turned around seeing that her mind was made up. Semaj put the gun to her temple and pulled the trigger again. Click!

This time she had to admit to herself that she was becoming a little afraid. Gomez looked on and was somewhat impressed that she had made it this far. Semaj finally took her eyes off of Gomez and looked at the gun. She popped the barrel out, spun it, and then slapped it back into the gun. Her palms became sweaty and her heart was racing. She looked at the gun again and then cocked the hammer back and pressed it up against her temple.

"You don't have to do it Maj," Sosa said, gripping her gun a little tighter.

If Semaj blew her own head off messing around with Gomez, Sosa had her mind made up that she was going to open fire on him anyway. She damn sure wasn't going to leave that tent without her, and neither was Gonzalez.

Semaj wrapped her finger around the trigger and in the time that it took Gomez to blink, Semaj turned the gun to Gomez and pulled the trigger. Boom! The last thing Gomez saw was the flash. The bullet hit him in the center of his forehead, knocking his body back into his chair. Gomez's two men were so shocked at what just happened that they hesitated before they could raise their guns to shoot. Sosa and Gonzalez didn't hesitate opening fire on the men.

The men outside weren't sure what to do or who

was doing the firing, so everybody had their guns aimed and ready to blast depending on who came out of the tent first. "Get in there! Get in there!' one of the guerrillas yelled out to the closest one by the entrance.

As he was going in, Gonzalez was coming out, guns blazing. He hit the guerrilla in his chest and then kept shooting. At this point everybody started shooting. Semaj and Sosa tried to run out of the tent behind Gonzalez but were met with gunfire that forced them to dive back inside.

"Shit! We gotta get out to the truck," Semaj yelled to Sosa over the loud gun battle outside.

She looked outside and could see a couple of her men falling to the ground. Others took cover behind the trucks but continued to return fire. Sosa and Semaj tried to go out the door but bullets tore holes in the tent right next to them. Semaj even heard a bullet whiz by her head.

"Shit!" Semaj yelled out.

There was a sigh of relief when the other three trucks pulled up in front of the tent. Semaj's men jumped out like SWAT giving the guerrillas hell.

"Semaaaj!...Sosaaa!" Gonzalez yelled for them to come out.

They both darted out of the tent but it seemed like when they did the gunfire got heavier. The truck was about twenty-five yards away but it felt like twenty-five miles. Bullets whizzed right overt their heads, and about halfway to the truck, one of those bullets hit Sosa in her leg, knocking her to the ground.

Semaj turned to go and help her but Gonzalez literally wrapped his arm around her waist, lifted her off of her feet and carried her the rest of the way to the truck. Semaj was kicking and screaming the whole time.

"Don't leave her! Don't leave her! Semaj yelled out as she was placed into the truck.

One of Gonzalez's men ran over to get Sosa. He scooped her up and started running towards the truck. Semaj looked out the window as her truck was pulling off. She watched as Sosa's carrier got within five yards of the truck and was hit twice in his back. He fell to the ground, dropping Sosa in the process. The driver of the truck tried to stay and help them but he began to take heavy gunfire, forcing him to make the choice of staying there and getting killed, or pulling off. He went with his first instinct and got out of the truck to try and help, but was bombarded with gunfire. He was hit several times before he could even get a shot off.

"Don't leave her! Don't leave her! Semaj yelled, as she banged on the window while her truck sped down the narrow road. The last thing that she saw before they exited the camp area was a few guerrillas running over and surrounding Sosa with large assault rifles in their hands.

Chapter 14

Qua stepped onto the hospital's elevator and pushed the number 6. He was curious to know why Murda Mitch was there and who he was there to see. He hadn't seen or heard from Semaj since the night at the club so he was somewhat worried that something had happened to her. Once on the 6th floor, Qua made his way down the hallway, cutting his eyes to look into every room that he passed by. It was when he got to the end of the hallway that he realized that he was probably on the wrong wing.

When he made the right at the end of the hall to go into the east-wing, he ran right into Vikingo's guards sitting outside of his room. He thought they were detectives because of the way they were dressed in suits. He walked past the room and cut his eyes in to see Murda Mitch standing there talking to the doctor about something. Qua knew then that it wasn't cops that were posted up. Qua didn't even get the chance to see who was lying in the bed.

"Damn! Qua mumbled to himself, seeing that the hallway led to a dead end.

That meant that he had to turn around and walk right back past Murda Mitch and hope that he could go unnoticed. The chances of that were slim, considering the fact that Mitch had just walked out of Vikingo's room and was standing in the hallway talking to the guards. Qua had no other choice but to expose himself.

"Yo, what up my nigga?" Mitch greeted, noticing Qua walking down the hall.

"Murda. What's good?" Qua responded, extending his hand. "Yeah, one of my boys got hit up pretty bad a couple of days ago. I just came through to check on him," Qua lied.

"Damn, is he okay?" Mitch asked, looking down the hallway in the direction Qua came from.

"Yeah, he's getting better, What's going on here?" Qua asked Mitch, nodding to Vikingo's room.

Mitch really didn't feel comfortable speaking on what went on with Vikingo and how Semaj had sent him to the States to get the proper medical treatment. He knew how much Qua loved his daughter and the last thing he wanted to do was get in the middle of a love triangle.

"Just visiting an old friend that is sick," Mitch said, as he started walking and trying to lead Qua away from the room.

As Qua was walking off, he took a peek into the room to see if it was somebody that he recognized. The many tubes running in and out of Vikingo's mouth and nose made it hard for Qua to identify him. He simply walked off with Mitch, relieved that it wasn't Semaj.

Paulette couldn't seem to figure out for the life of her where Sosa was and where she had taken Nyala. It was as if they had vanished off the face of the earth. She thought that Edna's death would bring Sosa out of hiding, but it didn't. Edna's body had begun stinking in Sosa's house, to the point neighbors had to cover their noses every time they walked past the house. It was only a matter of time before someone called the cops to report the foul odor.

Semaj rushed back home and returned to the jungle with a little more than two hundred armed men. They were ordered to kill everything and everyone moving who wasn't Sosa, and that's exactly what they did. Her men ran through that piece of land like a pack of wolves.

"Señorita!" Gonzalez yelled, coming from under one of the tents. "We checked every inch of this place and there is no sign of Sosa" he said, looking around the camp.

"Well keep looking," Semaj ordered, as she stood where she had seen Sosa being surrounded.

"Semaj!" Gonzalez said, calling her by her first name, something he rarely ever did. "I think that they took her, " he said, wiping the sweat from his brow.

"Took her?" What do you mean they took her?" she said, rising to her feet.

It was common for guerrillas to take captured men and women and turn them into slaves on a different coca plantation. Some women were even used as sex objects for the guerrillas to pounce upon whenever they felt like it, and if the women refused to have sex willingly, they would be raped, killed and then buried in the jungle.

Semaj looked around the camp trying to figure out where the guerrillas would have taken Sosa. The thing about Colombia is that it had jungles the size of Maryland, so there was no telling where she could have been. Whoever had Sosa already had a seven-hour head start and Semaj hadn't the slightest clue what direction they may have went. There were no roads that she could get on that would take her into the next camp, nor were there any maps to help her find her way. The jungle was the jungle, nothing but trees and bushes and some of the world's most venomous snakes.

"Señorita," let's go back home. These men can't stay out here much longer," Gonzalez said, looking around at the fatigued looks on their faces.

"I'm not leaving Sosa out here," Semaj replied, undeterred.

"I know some men that know these jungles very well. I give you my word that I will do everything in my power to find her. I promise that to you, Semaj," Gonzalez said, with his eyes full of sincerity.

Semaj didn't want to, but it seemed like she didn't' have any choice but to put her trust in Gonzalez. The men did look tired, plus the sun was starting to go down, a combination of two vital elements that were key to anybody's survival in the LeFedrera jungle.

Penny closed the coffee shop for the next couple of days so that she could get all of the cocaine they had in the basement to another location. Too much had been going on and the last thing Penny or Sosa needed was for the cops to run up in the shop.

Penny sat in the basement taking kilo after kilo from out of the deep freezer and placed it into a large duffle bag. She was going to have to make a few trips doing it this way but it was the only way that it was going to get done without drawing any attention to herself. Once the duffle bag was full, Penny locked the deep freezer and headed up the steps. An instant draft of air smacked her in the face when she got to the top of the steps, catching her attention. She looked out into the dark coffee shop and saw that the front door was wide open.

Penny pulled the 17 shot Glock 9mm from her waist and cautiously walked towards the front of the shop. She looked around as she passed by coffee tables and dining booths waiting for some type of movement to occur. She got closer and closer to the front of the coffee shop and for a moment, she forgot that she had a large duffle bag over her shoulder. Out of her peripheral view, Penny could see a shadow at the other end of the bar. She wasted no time in letting off a couple of shots in the shadow's direction.

It was a "shoot first and ask questions later" type of situation, and just when she was about to fire another shot, Paulette jumped out from behind the bar, letting off a few shots of her own. Penny turned and ran for the steps that led to the second floor, covering her face with her arm and hoping to avoid being shot in it. Paulette didn't stop there, she kept firing, chasing Penny up the steps with a family of hollow point bullets that knocked holes in the wall and steps. Two of the bullets would have hit Penny in her side but the duffle bag of cocaine saved her.

"Where you run to?" Paulette yelled, firing several more shots as she ran up the steps behind her.

Penny got to the second floor and immediately turned around and aimed her gun at the top of the steps. All she wanted was to see the top of Paulette's head pop up so she could send everything she had in her clip into her direction. She stood there and waited, but Paulette didn't come all the way up the steps.

The coffee shop became quiet for a moment, that is, until Penny heard Paulette drop the empty clip, slap another on in and cock her gun back. Penny fired a couple shots at the top of the steps anyway, just to let Paulette know that she had the upper hand.

"You don't have to die, little girl," Paulette yelled from the steps. "Just tell me where Sosa is," she said, trying to peek around the partition that separated the steps from the second floor.

Penny fired another shot, and missed hitting

Paulette in her head by two inches, knocking sheet rock from the partition on top of her. She was trying to kill Paulette, but her ammo was running short. Paulette was more than determined to find Sosa, and she was going to do it by all means necessary, even if that meant killing everybody Sosa knew.

"Awweee you bumba clot," Paulette said, reaching around the partition and firing several shots blindly onto the second floor.

Penny dipped off and fired another shot at her. Her gun felt light so she knew she was either out of bullets or close to it. "Shit!" she mumbled to herself trying to figure out what she was going to do.

She thought about her cell phone but when she reached for her pockets, she realized that her phone was sitting on the bar downstairs. "You gone die now," Paulette gloated.

Penny looked around the second floor and remembered there was a phone hanging up on the wall in the kitchen on the other side of the room. She took the duffle bag from around her neck and dropped it to the floor. She didn't need any weight holding her down as she darted across the room. She took off, racing across the room to the kitchen. Paulette could hear the fast but heavy footsteps running across the room. She poked her head out around the wall and fired several shots at Penny, striking her in her arm right before she dove into the kitchen.

Penny reached up and grabbed the cord to the

receiver of the phone, pulling it down. She dialed the first number that came to her mind, a number that she knew would get her the help that she needed. Penny simply dialed 911. The operator picked up on the first ring as expected.

"Help me please!" she screamed into the phone. "I've been robbed and shot," Penny continued.

Paulette heard that and became furious. She knew that she didn't have long before the cops responded. "Ahhhh," Paulette screamed coming up the steps and onto the second floor. She fired wildly into the kitchen at Penny who took refuge behind the refrigerator. Bullets knocked holes into the stainless steel box, all of which could be heard by the 911 operator who was still on the phone.

Penny fired back her last two rounds, striking Paulette in her midsection. It didn't penetrate the vest that she had on, but it knocked the wind out of her, buckling her to her knees. Penny saw that and took the opportunity to jump up from behind the refrigerator and run into the room. She began whaling on Paulette with several punches before grabbing the duffle bag and taking off down the steps. Paulette fired wildly into the direction of the steps, but didn't hit anything but the wall. She could hear the sounds of police sirens in the distance that prompted her to get to her feet and get down the steps.

Penny was already out the front door by the time Paulette made it down the steps. Paulette looked to the front of the coffee shop and could see nothing but red and blue lights flooding the streets, and Penny running out into the middle of the street flagging the cop cars down. She started to run out there and finish the job, but instead turned and headed for the back door, knowing that she could more than likely catch up with Penny again. On her way out she scooped up the large duffle bag Penny had tossed to the side, throwing it over her shoulder and pushing through the exit door.

Sosa woke up in pain. Her jaw hurt more than the bullet wound. She had been punched repeatedly by the guerrillas when she'd slowed them down while traveling through the jungle. Sosa looked around but her eyes weren't yet adjusted so everything was kind of a blur to her. She could hear the sound of laughter and men speaking Spanish right outside of the tent she was in. Then she heard a voice that was more clear and getting closer to her as she lay on the rocky ground.

"I gave you a sedative for the pain. The doctor will be here in a couple of hours to close up that wound," a man said, getting up from his chair in the back of the tent.

The voice sounded familiar to Sosa but she couldn't quite put a face to it. The image of a man walked up and squatted right in front of her, and as her eyes started to adjust she could see his face. She thought that she might have been imagining things when Raul's face became clear as day.

"Raul?" she asked with a prying but furious look on her face. He chuckled then reached over and cut the string that bound her wrists together.

"You know, you wasn't even suppose to get caught up in this, Sosa. The Espreilla Family has a way of pulling innocent people into their mess," he said, cutting the rope that bound her ankles together.

He was telling the truth. It wasn't about Sosa at all. It was about Semaj and had been since the day that she stepped up and became the head of the Espreilla Family.

"So what are you doing all of this for, Raul?" Sosa asked, rubbing her wrists and ankles.

"See, your cousin Semaj took on a whole other level of responsibility when she became the head of the family. Valentina murdered my brother in cold blood. He was hung, cut into pieces and delivered to different parts of my city."

"But Semaj didn't have nothing to do with that," Sosa cut in, vindicating her cousin.

"Just like the many people you killed that had nothing to do with Ox taking your daughter from you," Raul shot back. "Yes, I did my homework on you Sosa. You are a mean piece of work," he smiled.

Sosa had no words for that. When it came to Nyala she was willing to burn all Jamaica down and kill anybody that got in her way. She could see that the look Raul had in his eyes was the same look she'd had, and it was obvious that he was on a similar mission. Valentina might have died from natural causes but the want for revenge did not stop there. Semaj inherited more than just the family business. She inherited her grandmother's application for death by bullet and the man standing behind the gun was Raul Ordonez, brother of Julio Ordonez.

"So why haven't you killed me yet?" Sosa asked, looking down at the patch that covered the bullet wound to her leg.

"You're like my insurance policy in case things don't go as planned. I know your cousin will give just about anything for your safe return," Raul said, rising to his feet.

"And what plan is that?"

"The plan is to remove the Espreilla Family from the 16 Tent, and the only way that's going to get done is if I kill your cousin," he said, adjusting his clothes. "Oh, and while I'm at it, the Milano Family will no longer be a member of the Tent either."

Sosa tried to jump up but Raul punched her clean across her bruised chin, knocking her back down onto the ground. The pain of it shot through her whole body and it was as if the medication wore off instantly.

"Semaj is going to kill you," Sosa promised, spitting out a mouthful of blood. Raul looked at her and smiled.

"Not before I kill her first," he said boldly, and then walked out from under the tent.

Penny had a long night sitting trying to explain all the

events that took place in the coffee shop. Her biggest concern was keeping the detectives out of the basement where there were well over seventy kilos of cocaine in the freezer. She was a little hot when she realized that the Jamaican female had taken the duffle bag she'd placed by the basement door. Penny even told the detectives that Paulette had already left the shop, just so they wouldn't do too much searching around and possibly find the bag.

The detectives grilled her with question after question but Penny stood her ground and kept every answer short, sweet, and to the point. As she rode in the ambulance to the hospital, the only person she could think about was Sosa and where in the world she could be. This thing with the Jamaicans had certainly reached its height and Penny didn't have the slightest idea what to do except shoot to kill any Jamaican that posed a threat. That was going to be a task in and of itself because New York was full of them.

Chapter 15

Semaj's flight landed at the JFK Airport late in the afternoon. She had less than 24 hours until the 16 Tent meeting and had been awake for the past two days straight. The situation in Colombia was starting to take a toll on her and it didn't look like she was about to get to rest anytime soon, considering all of the running around the city she had to do. The first stop on her agenda was the hospital. She hadn't seen Vikingo since the day she sent him to New York and it ate her up that she hadn't been able to be by his side.

When she entered the hospital and found her way to his room, the two guards were sitting in chairs in outside his door. They both stood up like soldiers when they saw Semaj.

"Señorita," one of the men nodded, stepping to the side so that she could proceed inside the room.

"Go find me a doctor or a nurse," Semaj instructed the guard.

When she walked in and stood by his bedside, she grabbed his hand and placed it in hers gently. Tubes still ran through his nose and mouth helping him to breath. It didn't look like he was in any better shape than the last time she had seen him, but when he opened his eyes and looked up at Semaj, she knew that the doctors in Manhattan Medical had done their job.

"Ms. Espreilla?" the doctor asked, knocking on the door before entering.

Semaj couldn't manage a smile from the way she felt and the only real question she wanted to know was if he was going to make it.

"Well, Ms. Espreilla. The worst has passed and the surgery was successful. He is going to live; however, I am not sure if he is going to be able to walk again. The bullet did a lot of damage to the spinal cord. It was bruised pretty badly and he was unable to respond to the many nerve tests we did on him," the doctor explained.

"So you're saying he is paralyzed?" Semaj asked the doctor as she looked down on Vikingo who had closed his eyes.

"It's too early to tell whether or not it's going to be permanent, but for right now, he can't feel anything from his neck down."

It was like the doctor had hit Semaj with a baseball bat. The tears began to fill up her eyes as she imagined Vikingo not being able to walk again. It seemed like when it rained it poured. Nothing was going right in her life right now and Semaj was beginning to wonder whether she was not only built for this game but life in general.

"Maj!" Murda Mitch said, walking into the room.

She was relieved to see her father. Nobody had a clue about what was going on in Colombia and right now Mitch was the only person that Semaj could trust from the 16 Tent.

"What's the matter?" he asked, seeing the drained look in her eyes. "Vikingo is tough as nails. He'll make a full recovery just like I did."

"That's not the only thing Daddy. I got much bigger problems going on right now," Semaj whispered, pulling Mitch closer to her.

"Problems like what?"

She walked Mitch to the other side of the room so that the guards outside wouldn't be able to hear her. "Somebody in the 16 Tent wants me dead. They want to takeover my land."

Mitch didn't take too kindly to anybody trying to kill his seed. It didn't matter who you were, messing with his Princess was like begging for death. "Ima kill 'em," Mitch vowed, about ready to storm out of the room.

Semaj grabbed his arm and stopped him. She knew that he was two seconds away from blanking out. "Dad, I don't know who it is yet," Semaj revealed.

"Fuck it, I'ma kill 'em all!"

Semaj had to stop him because she knew that sure as water was wet, every member of the 16 Tent would be dead before the meeting that was scheduled for tomorrow morning. Something else had to be done and Semaj believed that one bad apple shouldn't spoil the bunch, it just needed to be picked out and thrown away. It was more important to keep these eight families intact, because together they controlled organized crime throughout the world. If the 16 Tent had any chance to be preserved, Semaj wanted to explore all of her options.

"I got a different idea Daddy," Semaj said, looking over at Vikingo. "Just let me quarterback this. I'ma find out exactly who it is," she assured him, before she walked out of the room.

Sosa lay on top of a table numb all over as the jungle doctor worked on her leg. An AK-47 bullet had ripped into her thigh and had not exited. It called for the doctor to have to go in and get it before it did anymore damage. Sosa could see everything that was happening but she couldn't feel shit. The jungle doctor extracted all of his medication from the jungle, and in all honesty, Sosa had to admit that the natural remedies he used were better than the stuff at the hospital, especially the yellow leaf that he used for pain.

The doctor dug into her leg like he was looking for buried treasure, using nothing but his two fingers and a pair of claws. Sosa could smell the blood and hear the sound of her flesh being moved around. She tried not to look down at the large hole in her leg. When she started to feel a little pain, she reached over, grabbed another leaf from the table and began chewing on it.

"Ni mas! Ni mas!" the doctor yelled, seeing that Semaj was eating too many of the leaves too fast.

He didn't want her body to get used to the plant, because after a while it wouldn't work anymore and the pain she would experience would be unbearable. She didn't understand; all she wanted was the instant relief. She prayed that he'd hurry up and get the bullet out of her leg.

Qua pulled up, parked in front of Semaj's hotel, and waited for her. No matter where they were in their relationship, whenever she needed Qua, he was going to be there for her, and right now she needed him bad. She actually needed all the help that she could get, but she only trusted a few.

Qua almost didn't notice Semaj when she walked out of the hotel dressed in a black, short-sleeved hoodie, blue jeans, and a pair of black and red Jordans. She was on some hood shit; the only way he recognized her was by the way she walked. Qua would know her strut anywhere. She walked right over to the Benz and hopped into the passenger side.

"Damn Ma, what's really good wit' you?" Qua said, looking over at Semaj, who was hiding her face under her hood.

"Pull off," she responded, keeping her head sunken in the seat.

Qua didn't ask another question. He pulled off, looking in his rearview mirrors like he was being followed. Semaj had him feeling paranoid, but all she was trying to do was leave the hotel without being noticed by her own security. Had they known she was going outside, they would have insisted on coming with her. That was something she wanted to avoid right now.

"Maj, what da hell is going on?" Qua asked, looking over at her.

Semaj slowly took the hood off of her head, flipped down the sun visor and began fixing her hair. "Qua, it's some shit goin' down right now and I really need your help." she said, looking out the rearview to make sure they weren't being followed.

Semaj began telling Qua the intricate details of everything she was dealing with. She told him about the poachers, Vikingo being shot and paralyzed by a group of guerrillas, and the fact that somebody from the 16 Tent wanted her dead. She told him about how she ran through Colombia putting in work, trying to find out who was setting her up. She even broke down into tears when she told Qua about Sosa, and how she was still in the jungle somewhere wounded, and no one was even sure if she was dead or alive.

This was the first time Semaj had been allowed to be completely vulnerable and release all of her built up emotions. Qua was the only person she felt comfortable crying around without having to fear that she would be perceived as weak.

"So, how do you wanna do this?" Qua asked, after listening carefully to every word Semaj said. He already knew how he thought it should go down, but in his mind the most important thing was just getting it done, because he hated to see Semaj in this much pain. Qua was so furious he had to pull over before he ended up crashing.

"We have a Tent meeting tomorrow morning..."

"Fuck it, lets kill 'em all," Qua suggested, cutting Semaj off.

His mind was pretty much made up from the moment Semaj told him that one of the members tried to have her killed. Anybody that posed that kind of threat had to be dealt with immediately. Semaj had to explain the same thing to him as she did to her father about the importance of the Tent families and how she just wanted to get rid of the bad apple.

"Well, if we can't kill them all just tell me who you want me to kill so I can get this shit over wit'," Qua said.

Semaj looked over at him. She could see the genuine love he had for her. It was written all over his face. It made her smile, something she hadn't been able to do for what seemed like forever. The way Qua was quick to step up, ready to protect her, made it seem just like old times as they sat there in the car. Old memories of how deep their friendship and love ran flooded her mind. Semaj wanted to confess that she was still very much in love with him and had missed him over the past year or so, but now wasn't the best time to do it, especially with Vikingo being in his condition.

Snap! Snap! Snap! "Semaj!" Qua said, snapping his fingers and breaking her train of thought. "So what you wanna do?" he asked, looking for her to say something.

"Right now, I need you to help me do some homework. I got a funny feeling that whoever it is that wants me dead will show his true colors tomorrow. We just got to apply the right pressure to the right person," Semai said, as she stared out the window at the Times Square lights beaming in the dark.

The jungle doctor managed to get most of the bullet fragments out of Sosa's leg before patching it up with a special mud that helps wounds heal faster. It was evident that the yellow leaves were wearing off because Sosa was in a nice bit of pain. The jungle doctor prescribed her green berries to help with the pain, warning her by a show of his hands not to eat too many of them.

As the doctor was leaving, Sosa attempted to grab a small knife he had in his kit, but she was unsuccessful. She desperately needed that knife, because the whole time the doctor was working on her leg, she could hear a conversation that was going on between the two guards that were standing watch outside of her tent. Nobody really knew that Sosa could speak Spanish and she kept it that way for a reason, hoping that people would talk freely and reveal a way out of the jungle. Instead of hearing that, Sosa overheard the two men arguing about who was going to have sex with her first, after her leg healed up enough. These rebels were crazy in every sense of the word, and the lack of female companions out in the jungle made Sosa too tantalizing to pass up.

Qua made it back to Semaj's hotel after driving around the city all night. By the time he pulled in front of the hotel, Semaj was asleep, curled up in the passenger seat. He nudged her but she didn't move. From his experience of sleeping next to her in bed at night, there was no waking her up.

He nudged her one last time but it was like she curled up even tighter in the seat. Qua couldn't do anything but smile. She looked so beautiful to him. Now, he was given the option to lift her up, take her into the hotel, find her security so they could take her to her room, or he could simply take her home with him and bring her back in the morning after she got a few hours of sleep. For Qua, it was a no brainer. He looked over at Semaj, threw the Benz in drive and pulled off.

Penny pulled up to Sosa's house hoping that she could find some kind of answers as to where Sosa was. She'd had enough of dealing with the Jamaicans and was pretty much blind to the history behind the whole situation. When she got out of the car and looked to the front door, she could see that it was slightly cracked open. Penny thought that looked suspicious, so she reached back under the driver's seat, grabbed the compact .45 automatic, and proceeded to the house.

The closer she got the more she could smell a vicious

stench coming from the house. She couldn't identify it, but it was beginning to smell so bad that she had to put her hand over her nose. It only got worse when Penny opened the door, and when she looked into the house, it was clear where the smell was coming from.

Edna's body was visibly lying in the middle of the living room covered in blood. Feces and urine were also clearly noticeable. "Fuck!" Penny mumbled to herself holding her nose as she walked up closer to the body.

She couldn't tell from a distance who it was. She had to make sure that it wasn't Sosa lying there so she walked over to it. Her heart raced in fear thinking it might have been Sosa, but when she got up close she breathed a sigh of relief realizing that it wasn't.

At the same time, she felt bad for Edna, who she knew very well from the many times Penny came over to Sosa's for dinner or just to chill out. *Damn Sosa, where the hell are you?* Penny walked through the entire house with her gun in hand to make sure Sosa wasn't in one of the other rooms dead herself. Once Penny was done, she pulled out her cell phone and dialed 911.

Chapter 16

"You know, our friend is getting stronger," Marco told Nikolai as they sat in the hotel dining hall eating breakfast.

He heard about how hard Semaj was going in Colombia taking over the local cartel groups. Word like that traveled fast, especially when a family as large as the Espreilla Family was reestablishing power in their city.

"I think we both know what needs to be done before this situation gets out of hand," Nikolai urged, as she took a sip of his coffee.

She was referring to killing Raul so that none of this would have the chance to backfire on her and Marco. She'd underestimated Semaj and didn't think that she was going to be strong enough to fight back, but with every day that passed, she was building strength. The kind of strength that could be dangerous to her enemies, and even somebody so wicked, so vicious, and so ruthless and Nikolai knew that they wouldn't stand a chance going up against her.

"I'm going upstairs to get ready for this meeting. Hopefully by the time we have it our friend Raul won't be around," Marko said, as he got out of his chair and headed out of the dining hall.

"I'll take care of it," Nikolai said, as she took another sip of her coffee, then reached into her bag for her cell phone.

Semaj could hear Qua's voice before she even opened her eyes. He was on his cell phone in the next room yelling at one of his workers. When Semaj finally did open her eyes, she looked around and was impressed with the interior design of the room. The brown baseboards complemented the cocaine-white walls and the 18-foot high ceiling had a cabin-style fixture to it. Semaj sat up in what seemed to be a super king-size bed with a custom oak headboard that had sculpted tiger designs. The space was so huge it had a section of it that looked like a separate living room.

"Damn," Semaj mumbled to herself, looking over at the clock on the nightstand. It was already 9:30 and the meeting was in two hours. She climbed from underneath the blanket fully clothed except for the hoodie that was replaced by one of Qua's t-shirts. He walked into the room just as she was getting out of the bed.

"Look who's awake," Qua smiled. "I was just about to come and wake you up."

Semaj was exhausted last night and she was still a little tired even after getting close to eight hours of sleep.

"Towels and wash cloths are in the bathroom along

with new soap, toothpaste and a new toothbrush. It's gonna take us about half hour to get to Manhattan so you can take your time," he said, walking over to the large walk-in closet.

"I don't have shit to wear. You gotta take me back to the hotel," she said, walking over to the vanity mirror in the corner.

"Come here," he said, nodding his head.

Semaj walked over to the closet and looked around. He had all kinds of clothes in it. There were so many options it looked like a mini men's boutique. Qua got on the small ladder, reached up to the top shelf, and grabbed a mid-sized box. Semaj just stood there with a curious look on her face.

"Don't be tryin' to give me none of your old girlfriends' clothes," Semaj joked.

Qua chuckled a bit, and then opened the box. "I was saving this hoping that one day you would come back to me," he said, pulling out a couple of pairs of jeans and a couple of shirts wrapped in plastic. Semaj grabbed the items and damn near broke into tears. She knew off the break that these were her old clothes from when her and Qua were living together.

"Remember this?" he smiled, pulling out a teddy bear.

Semaj laughed and grabbed it, kissing it on the nose. She could never forget Baby Jake, the teddy bear they used to keep in the bed with them and play like it was their baby. Semaj couldn't believe that Qua still had it. She looked at him, and for few seconds they had a moment. Qua broke the stare, feeling himself starting to get aroused.

"I know the clothes are a little outdated, but you can make anything look good," he said, grabbing the teddy bear out of Semaj's hand and placing it back in the box.

Semaj hated that Qua had this kind of effect on her. When she was around him, he was all she needed. She felt a sense of completion in her life with Qua, a feeling she never had with any other man, and every second that she sat in his presence, her feelings for him began to resurface at an alarming rate. As much as Semaj wanted to give into these feelings, she knew right now she had to focus on the current situation with 16 Tent and Sosa.

Penny walked right up to the unmarked car and tapped on the passenger side window. Agent Davis looked out the window with an angry glare. He acted like he wasn't going to roll the window down so Penny knocked on it again, this time a little bit harder than the last. Davis gave her the same look, but this time the window came down.

"What do you want?" he said, with an attitude not even acknowledging her with direct eye contact.

Penny had an attitude of her own and didn't hesitate giving Davis a piece of her mind. "How is it that you sit here and watch my establishment all day but the cops can't seem to figure out who shot up my place of business?" Penny snapped. "Who are ya'll? The feds? Detectives?"

Penny couldn't get another word out before the Agent pulled off on her. She was starting to make a scene and they weren't going to sit around and let her draw attention to them. "Mutha Fuckas!" she yelled out, watching them drive off.

Penny was red hot about the entire situation but at the same time she was worried as hell about Sosa whom she hadn't seen or heard from in a few days. She didn't know if she was alive or dead and being as though Sosa kept her circle tight, it wasn't too many people she could call to find out where she was, and the few people Sosa did kick it with, was calling Penny looking for answers.

On her way up to the coffee shop, Penny pulled out her phone and decided to call the one person Sosa told her to get in touch with in case of an emergency. She scrolled through her phone until she came upon Semaj's number. Penny knew Semaj, just not on a personal level, but from the way Sosa use to brag about her and say how much she loved her cousin, Penny had a great deal of respect for her. She also knew that Semaj was the only family that Sosa had besides her daughter, and Sosa had told Penny that if anything was to happen to her, call Semaj.

Penny pushed 'Talk' and then put the phone in front of her face as it began to ring. It took a few rings, but Semaj finally answered. "Who's this?" Semaj asked when she answered.

"Can I speak with Semaj?"

"Yeah, this is she. Who's this?" Semaj asked again,

while looking out the passenger window of Qua's Benz.

"Semaj, this is Penny. I work for Sosa."

"I know who you are, Penny. I was wondering when you were going to call me." Once she said her name, Semaj knew exactly who she was. Sosa spoke highly of Penny, something she rarely ever did with anybody.

"It's been a few days and Sosa hasn't been to the shop, nor did she call me. I'm concerned."

"I know Penny. We got a small situation. I was wondering if we could meet up and talk," Semaj said, looking out onto the highway.

From the way Sosa described Penny, she figured that she could use her help. If she was going to find out where Sosa was, she was going to need all the help she could get.

"Yeah we can meet up. I need to talk to you about something else too," Penny said, looking into the bullet-riddled coffee shop. "Come by the coffee shop. I can show you better then I could explain it to you," Penny said before hanging up the phone.

Semaj sat in deep thought after getting off of the phone with Penny. There was so much going on in her life right now and she honestly didn't know how her story was going to end. One thing that she was confident about was that if it were the end of her reign, she would go out with guns blazing.

"Thank you," she looked over and told Qua, who was concentrating on the traffic.

"For what?"

"For helping me. I know you don't have to be here..."

"Stop!" Qua said, cutting her off. "Don't do that to me, Maj. Don't talk to me like we just met or some shit like that," Qua semi-snapped. "If you think I'ma sit back and let some shit happen to you, you really don't know me," he said, pulling up to the red light.

Qua had a lot of built up, unresolved feelings regarding the way their relationship had ended. There wasn't a day that went by he didn't think about her and what his life would have been like if they were still together. It had affected him to the point that he didn't want to give his heart to anyone else.

"Listen Maj, I'm not gonna lie to you," he said, turning to face her. "I still love you. To be honest wit' you I probably love you more now than I ever did," he confessed. "You was my world, and ever since the day we split up, my life has been filled with nothing but regret."

"Don't do this right now, Qua. Please don' do this now," Semaj pleaded, holding back the urge to say the things that had been on her mind for a long time too.

"I miss you Maj," Qua said, reaching over and placing his hand on top of hers.

Semaj looked at him and could see the sincerity in his eyes. She wanted to lean over and kiss him, and tell him that everything was going to be perfect between them, but she couldn't. As much as she loved Qua and wanted nothing more but to be with him, the issue still remained that she also loved Vikingo. It wasn't the same love that she had for Qua, but nonetheless, she loved him and wasn't about to leave him, especially now that he might be paralyzed for the rest of his life.

The light had turned green, but Qua was so caught up in the moment that he didn't even realize he was holding up traffic. Cars started blowing their horns behind him, snapping him out of their intense gaze.

"Maj, I am never going to give up on us," he said, as he began to pull off.

Wwwhaaam!

Just as Qua was pulling off, a car came from out of nowhere and smacked into the front drivers side fender, spinning the Benz 180 degrees into the intersection. Both the passenger- and the driver-side airbags deployed.

Stunned, but still conscious, Semaj pushed the airbag out of her face. She looked out into the street and could see shadows running towards the car. Things were still fuzzy but became a little clearer when the sun's rays bounced off a chrome gun in the hands of one of the shadows running towards her.

Pop! Pop! Pop!

Qua sent three quick shots out of Semaj's window into the direction of the gunman, striking him somewhere in his upper body. Semaj reached under her seat, grabbed a Glock 9mm, and then bailed out of the car. Qua bailed out and was met with immediate gunfire by another gunman who exited the car that had crashed into them. He got low to the ground and ran to the back of the car where Semaj had taken refuge.

"It's a hit!" Qua yelled out over the heavy gunfire coming their way.

"How many of them are there?" Semaj asked, clutching her gun tightly and flinching from the bullets hitting the car.

"I don't know!" he shouted back, reaching around the car and firing several shots.

The sounds of a pair of thick tires coming to a screeching halt in the middle of the intersection got Semaj's attention. She could hear men yelling at each other in Spanish as they jumped out of the vehicle.

"Kill both of them!" one of the gunmen yelled.

Hearing that, Semaj hopped up in the midst of all of the bullets being fired her way, and began shooting at what she now saw was an SUV that had pulled into the intersection. The three men that got out of it took refuge behind it. Qua hopped up too, fearlessly throwing shots back at the first set of gunmen. Qua needed to get to his trunk bad. He walked to the driver-side door of his car, all the while firing single shots at the gunmen. He ran out of bullets the second he was about to lean in and hit the trunk button.

"Shit!" he shouted, tossing the gun to the side.

He reached in, pushed the trunk button, and then darted to the back of the car. Semaj was right there covering him, firing several rounds. The gunmen from both vehicles began to spread out into the street around Qua's Benz. Cars from both sides of the intersection were at a standstill. Nobody wanted to move and everybody's heads were sunk below their dashboards. Surprisingly, there wasn't a single cop in sight.

"Stay by my side," Qua told Semaj as he lifted the trunk all the way open.

He reached in and lifted the whole floor of the trunk up, tossing the light plastic floorboard into the street. Gunfire from the assassins erupted again. Qua grabbed his AR-15 from his stash spot while Semaj wrapped her hands around two twin .45 automatics and cocked a bullet into the head of both of them. Qua came from behind the car with Semaj at his side. He opened fire with the large assault rifle, forcing everybody to get low, even the civilians stuck at the intersection in their cars.

The targets were spread out, so Semaj fired in one direction and Qua fired in the other. They stood side by side blasting away, giving the hitmen hell. Through all of the gunfire, police sirens could finally be heard in the distance. The gunmen continued to fire shots as they retreated to the SUV. Then, one of the men from the car had that crashed into Qua tried to make a break for the SUV, since his car was out of commission.

Semaj saw him darting across the street, so she spun around and began shooting at him. She fired shots from both of the .45s, striking him in his shoulder and in the side of his head.

"We gotta go!" Qua yelled to Semaj.

The rest of the men jumped into the SUV and sped off, but not before Qua finished the remainder of the clip, sending several more bullets into the blue Expedition.

Bullets hit the side of it and shattered the back glass. Qua ran to the driver's side but quickly realized the damage that his car had sustained from the crash wasn't going to allow him to drive. It wasn't just his fender that was damaged. His whole front wheel was bent in and was damn near off the axle.

He looked up and could see the flashing lights approaching. Other cars were brave enough to start pushing through the intersection trying to get away from the crime scene before the police started taping off the streets.

"Come on!" Qua yelled, grabbing Semaj by her arm and running with her through the heavy traffic in the opposite direction than the cops were coming from. By the time the police cars pulled into the intersection, Semaj and Qua were a little more than a block away. What gave them even more distance from the cops was the fact that most of the police cars were responding to shots being fired from a blue SUV and there were reports of an officer down.

Apparently, the last round of bullets from Qua's gun had hit the driver. The SUV crashed a few blocks away and a small shootout ensued between the occupants of the SUV and a patrol officer walking the beat.

"I got to get you somewhere safe," Qua told Semaj as he hurried down the street with her in tow.

Semaj snatched her arm away from him and stopped in mid-stride.

"I'm not goin' anywhere Qua," she said, in a frustrated tone.

"What do you mean? They almost killed you just now," he yelled at her.

"Look Qua, I am not running. I am not hiding from nobody. We're gonna stick to the plan like I said. If you wanna back out that's fine with me. But I am goin' to the conference and I'ma find out who's behind this. And when I find them, they will die," she said, walking past Qua and heading for the subway.

Qua had seen this type of determination before in Semaj and he knew that he only had two choices: either ride with her or get left behind. It was something Qua didn't even have to think about. If he had to, he would ride to the end of the world with Semaj without question. As she headed down the subway steps on 8th Avenue, Qua took a look around on the street level and then jogged down the steps right behind her.

"Room service!" the housekeeper yelled, tapping on Raul's hotel room door.

Raul looked up from the laptop as he sat at the table asking himself why room service would be at his door, since they had already cleaned the room this morning. He was 100% sure that he hadn't ordered any food, so the more the maid tapped on the door, the more suspicious he became.

"Room service!" the housekeeper announced again, this time sliding the master key into the door and opening it slightly.

Raul got up from the table before the door could open all the way and dipped off into the bedroom. The female maid reached under her skirt, pulled a Hi-Point 9mm Luger, screwed a silencer onto it, and proceeded to enter the room. She kept the gun pointed in front of her as she cautiously looked around the room. Raul watched through a crack in the bedroom door as the maid walked through the other room.

He tippy-toed over to his suitcase, reached in and grabbed his chrome .40 caliber Smith and Wesson, then slowly walked over and stood against the wall behind the door. He stayed still and waited silently for the bedroom door to open. When it finally opened, Raul pressed the .40 caliber up against the door and pulled the trigger. The bullet went through the door and directly into the maid's head.

Her body dropped to the ground right in the threshold of the door. Raul opened the door all the way, looking down at the hole on the side of her head that had blood oozing out of it. He had a feeling that Nikolai and Marco were going to try to kill him eventually, he just didn't know that it was going to be this soon. Without thinking twice, Raul grabbed his suitcase, threw all of his clothes into it, took his laptop off the table and walked right out of the room without looking back.

Chapter 17

The longer Paulette stayed in New York the more she began to like the city and all that it had to offer. She had thought the bag that she'd taken from Penny at the coffee shop would have something in it leading her to Sosa's whereabouts, but when she saw it contained 15 bricks of cocaine, it changed a lot of things. She'd heard that Sosa was making moves in the States, but not like this. And if she had 15 bricks of cocaine in her coffee shop, Paulette figured there might have been a whole lot more to her brothers' baby momma than she knew.

"Yo, me can get 25k easy for each key," Patrick said, walking up and taking a seat next to Paulette in the booth.

Paulette had found refuge at one of her brother's clubs in Jamaica Queens that was run by an old friend of Ox. Even after his death, Ox still had a lot of people in check, along with a lot of businesses that were unclaimed. These were some of the benefits Paulette was running into during her stay.

"Dat's almost a half million," Paulette said, looking over at Patrick in shock.

She knew about the coke game from her brother but she'd never really gotten into it deep enough to know the prices of the product. To hear those kinds of numbers gave her reason to smile.

"And what about the other thing?" she asked, talking about the private investigator she had hired to find Sosa.

"Me looked everywhere and there is no sign of her or Nyala. She must have taken her somewhere far," Patrick informed her regrettably. "The private investigator even gave me money back," he said, reaching into his pocket and pulling out a wad of money. "I think that we should take the money that we get from the drugs and go back to Jamaica until we can find her again," Patrick suggested.

"No, no, me not goin' nowhere," Paulette shot back. "Me gon' stay right here in New York until I find me niece. I know Sosa be back. I know it, I know it, I know it," she said adamantly, banging her fist on the table.

The few workers that were in the club looked over to see what all the commotion was about, but quickly got back to work once they saw it was Paulette.

"So you wanna stay here?" Patrick asked.

It wasn't that long ago Paulette used to tell him how much she hated the States and how messed up it was that some of their people turned their backs on Jamaica to live there. To hear her say that she was going to stay was weird to him, but for Paulette it was a sacrifice that needed to be made for more than one reason, and Nyala was at the top of her agenda.

"We stay until Sosa come back. We make her tink

that everting die down. And when she do come back we be ready for her," Paulette said, before ending the conversation and turning her attention to the TV that was hanging up in the corner of the V.I.P section.

The security was heavy outside of the ballroom in the Four Seasons where the conference was supposed to take place. Members usually brought their own form of security and that's what made every 16 Tent meeting safe. Nikolai, Marco Dedaj, and the Nigerian couple were the first to show up to the meeting. Ezra and his wife sat at one end of the extra large, marble oval round table, while Nikolai and Marco sat at the other end holding somewhat of a pre-conference before everybody else showed up.

"Did you take care of our problem?" Marco asked, leaning in to talk so nobody could hear his conversation with Nikolai.

"I made the call this morning. More than likely we are going to have an empty seat today," Nikolai said, lighting the long, white cigarette between her fingers. "Have you heard anything about Semaj?" she asked, after taking the first drag of the nicotine stick.

Marco just shook his head. He hadn't heard anything at all from Semaj and was actually starting to think that Raul had made good on his promise. "Hopefully we will have two seats empty today," Marco answered, sitting back in his chair.

As always, Wong Won entered the room in a chipper

mood, walking around smiling and shaking everybody's hand. Murda Mitch came in right behind him, but he wasn't in a good mood at all, so he didn't even speak to anybody. He just took his seat right next to where Semaj was supposed to be seated and waited.

A small bit of commotion outside in the hallway caught everyone's attention, but by the time Marco got up to see what it was all about, Semaj came walking through the door, passing off the twin .45's to the security.

"Sit down," Semaj told Marco, pointing to his chair as she walked around the table to where her chair was.

Marco eyed Semaj like she was crazy for speaking to him like that, but he did what he was told. Semaj was looking rough. Her hair was sweated out, clothes disheveled, and she had scrapes on her arms from her dive behind the Benz during the assassination attempt. Nikolai just put her head down in disappointment.

"Maj, what the fuck happened to you?" Mitch asked, getting up out of his seat.

"I got it," she answered, whispering to him.

Semaj looked around the room and into the eyes of each and every person sitting at the table. Ezra and his wife looked more concerned for Semaj than anything, so she was able to rule the Nigerian couple out first. Next was Wong Won, who had a baffled expression on his face as he looked around at everybody else.

"Someone tried to kill me this morning," Semaj said, as she stood there leaning up against the table with her fist balled up.

"What!" Mitch shouted, jumping up from his seat. "Who was it?" he asked, through clenched teeth.

Semaj looked around the room again. The whole atmosphere changed this time. She focused her attention on Marco, who was looking right back at her with a stone glare on his face.

"Why would somebody want to kill you, Semaj?" Marco asked, sitting up in his chair.

Before she could even try to answer that question, Raul came walking through the door. He froze for a split second, seeing that Semaj was still alive. He thought that his people took care of her this morning. He should have known that something went wrong when he didn't get a phone call from his top gunmen that led the hit.

"Am I late?" Raul asked, taking a seat at his chair.

"No, you're right on time," Nikolai said, staring at him with the same disappointing look on her face that she had when Semaj came walking through the door. "Semaj just finished telling us that somebody tried to kill her this morning," she said, as she put out her cigarette.

Raul sat in his chair with a blank stare on his face. There was a moment of awkward silence in the room. Marco sat there with his head down while Nikolai lit up another cigarette. Semaj could feel how thick the shade and negativity was coming from the side of the table where Nikolai, Marco, and Raul sat. None of them could even look at Semaj. She didn't know which one of them were responsible but she knew one if not all three had something to do with it.

"You know, killing a member of the 16 Tent without the consensus of all of the members is a crime punishable by death," Wong Won said, looking around the room. "I guess this issue is going to be at the top of our meeting today. So where's Sosa?" Wong Won asked, wanting to get the meeting started.

"She will be here in a few minutes. Unfortunately, she was kidnapped while she was in Colombia. She escaped her captors this morning and is now on a flight back here as we speak," Semaj answered.

Ezra and his wife immediately showed concern along with Won asking a million and one questions. Semaj lied about Sosa because she was curious to see the reaction of the three people she had on her suspect list. Immediately following those words panic seemed to engulf Raul's entire face. He tried to quickly cover it up but it was too late, Semaj had already seen his true colors. She didn't draw any attention to it, but rather put it into her memory box. Nikolai seemed kind of suspicious as well, which got Semaj to really start thinking.

"I think that we should all take a break and resume the meeting once Sosa's plane lands, which should be any minute now. We'll meet back here in two hours." Semaj said.

"Good, 'cause I can use a drink," Ezra said, grabbing his wife by the hand and leading her out of the room.

Semaj sat down in her chair and interlocked her fingers together on the bait that she had just thrown out there, and one by one people started to get up from the table and leave the room.

Sosa grabbed a handful of dirt and threw it into the face of one of the rebels that entered the tent in another attempt to rape her. He charged at her as he was trying to wipe the dirt out of his eyes, grabbing her with his free hand and throwing her up against the wooden desk at the back of the tent. He was strong as hell but Sosa kept fighting.

"Stop moving!" the rebel yelled, smacking her across the face with the back of his hand.

Sosa kept swinging punch after punch, grabbing stuff off the desk and hitting him with it, screaming at the top of her lungs. It was as if none of that fazed him, because somehow through the fighting and struggling, he managed to pull Sosa's pants off.

"No! No! No! Please don't!" Sosa begged, feeling herself running out of energy.

The rebel could feel Sosa getting weaker. He ripped her panties clean off, reached into his pants and pulled out his dick. In her last attempt to stop him from raping her, Sosa used every bit of strength she could muster and reached down grabbing a hold of the tip of his dick before he could push it into her. He tried to pull back but Sosa had a nice amount of it in her hand and wasn't going to let go for nothing.

"Aaarrrgggg!" he yelled, as she dug her nails into the head of his dick.

Sosa reached up with her free hand and dug her thumb into his eye. He jerked his head back, made a fist and punched Sosa in her face. He punched her and punched her over and over again until he just about knocked her out. Sosa's grip loosened up on his dick enough for him to get it out of her hand.

"You crazy bitch!" the rebel shouted, looking down at the bruises she left on his penis.

He couldn't stick his dick into Sosa even if he still wanted to. It had shriveled up and looked like a turtle going into its shell. He grabbed his falling pants and stumbled out of the tent. Two other rebels that were standing right outside the whole time the assault was happening were laughing at him because he came out with all kinds of scratches on his face. He felt so humiliated that he grabbed the AK-47 he'd left leaning up against the side of the tent and attempted to go back in and shoot her.

"Whoa! We can't kill her," one of the rebels yelled, sticking his arm out and stopping the man at the entrance. "Go walk it off," he advised him with a stern look.

He did just that, storming off down the dirt road. Sosa rolled off the desk and fell to the ground. She crawled over to her pants and struggled to put them back on. Her whole body was in pain and she could feel the entire right side of her face swelling up. She didn't know how much longer she could endure these vicious attacks, but she would do it until death, or at least until she could not fight any longer.

Chapter 18

Penny went to the hotel Raul had been staying at, only to find cops everywhere. They weren't letting anyone in or out of the hotel no matter who you were. She walked up to a crowd of people standing in front of the hotel.

"Yo, what happened?" she asked one of the hotel staff standing off to the side.

"Somebody got shot," the female answered, pointing to the coroner rolling the dead body through the lobby.

"Did they catch the person responsible?" Penny asked, looking at a group of detectives huddled up in the lobby sharing notes.

"No. From what I heard, nobody saw anything. The cops are looking at the surveillance tapes now," the woman answered, only telling Penny what her fellow worker that was still inside had told her.

The thing about members from the 16 Tent, they were like ghosts. Nobody ever used his or her real names for anything, especially when traveling. The room Raul used wasn't in his name, and the only thing police had to go off of was the surveillance photos from the hotel. Penny quickly whipped out her cell phone to call Semaj. She wasn't sure, but Penny had a gut feeling that the murder had something to do with everything that was going on.

Raul walked out into the courtyard, debating on whether or not to call his contact in the jungle to check and see what happened to Sosa. There were a couple of people sitting at the little tables but he wasn't paying them any attention. His mind was too consumed on Sosa. He couldn't believe that she had somehow gotten away and was headed back to the States. He paced back and forth a few times before finally deciding to call. The phone call was going to determine the next chain of events that was going to take place, because if she really had escaped and was on her way back to the States, Semaj was going to find out that he was the one behind everything. That was a guaranteed death sentence, but Raul being who he was, he wasn't going to just lie down and die. If he was going to go out, he was going to go out with a bang.

Raul looked through the window back into the lobby to make sure nobody from the Tent was going to come out where he was. He noticed that Nikolai and Marco were having somewhat of a heated discussion by the bar.

"I'll deal with you two in a minute," he mumbled to

himself as he pulled out his phone.

Nikolai and Marco trying to kill him wasn't going to go unanswered either, Raul had decided. The shocked looks on their faces when he walked into the meeting unscathed sealed their guilt.

"Hola Señor," Barbosa, the Lieutenant of the rebels answered.

"Como demonios dejaste que la chica de escape?" Raul questioned with his voice full of anger, as he kept a sharp eye on Nikolai and Marko.

"The girl is still here," Barbosa answered, looking into the tent where Sosa was lying down.

Raul looked into the sky and then back down at the phone before hanging it up. It took him a second, but he figured out that Semaj was setting him up. He went back into his phone to try to erase Barbosa's number, but before he could, Qua jumped up from one of the tables, walked over and jammed a .40 caliber into his back.

"Push another button and I'ma push a button of my own," Qua warned, reaching around and easing the phone out of Raul's hand.

"So now what? You plan on shooting me right here, with all of these cameras hanging up everywhere?" Raul said in a calm voice.

"No, I'm not gonna shoot you. But we gone take a little walk," Qua said, as he patted Raul down and removed the gun he had on his waist.

Craaaackk!

Qua hit Raul so hard in the back of his head with

his gun, Raul blanked out for a second. He didn't realize that he was knocked out while still standing up until he came to. Things were a little fuzzy but he saw the serious look Qua had on his face.

"Alright, alright," Raul complied, pressing down on the knot that had instantly popped up on his head.

"Now move," Qua demanded, pushing Raul in his back to go back into the hotel.

"You said that this wasn't going to come back on us," Marco angrily whispered to Nikolai as he unbuttoned his blazer.

"And it won't," Nikolai answered, trying to assure him. "Let me just make another call."

"No. No more phone calls. I think you should get out of here before it's too late," Marco suggested.

"Get out of here?" she shot back. And what about you?" Nikolai asked, like he didn't have anything to worry about.

"If they ask me any questions I'm going to deny everything. My words hold more weight than you think," Marco said, and then walked off.

He wasn't lying either. Marco had been a member of the 16 Tent since it began, not like everybody else who came years later, or may have inherited their spots. To touch somebody like Marco you would have to have strong proof of him violating the rules and regulations of the Tent. Just word of mouth wasn't going to be enough, and Marco knew that.

Semaj walked into the hotel room where Qua told her to meet him. She was finishing up her phone conversation with Penny when she walked through the door but quickly ended the call once she saw Raul sitting on the bed.

"For someone who tried to kill me, you sure don't look worried right now," Semaj said, seeing the look of calmness on Raul's face.

"He made the call," Qua said, walking over and giving her the phone. "He said some shit in Spanish so I don't know what he was talking about."

Semaj took the phone and began scrolling through his phone book. She walked over and took a seat on the bed right next to Raul, inhaling a deep breath then exhaling slowly. Raul turned to face her and then cracked a smile.

"Is this the part where you become all gangsta on me?" he mocked, raising one eyebrow. "Cause if it is you can save the act. I know you're not gonna touch me, Semaj."

"Yeah, why is that?" she asked, turning to face him.

"It's simple. If you kill me, you will never find Sosa. You might have my phone, but who's gonna call my guys and tell them to let her go ... this guy?" he said, nodding in Qua's direction.

"No, no, no, You're gonna call," Semaj said, passing him his phone.

Her calm demeanor was unexpected by Raul and he wondered what tricks she had up her sleeve. He had already prepared himself to be tortured and killed the moment Qua put that gun to his back in the courtyard, but he also had plans on escaping by using Sosa as a negotiation tool.

"The only way I'll call is if I walk out of this door. Other than that, my men have strict instructions to put a bullet in your cousin's head if I don't return to the jungle in two days, and I told them that yesterday. So it's totally up to you how the story ends," Raul smirked, as he brushed some lint off his pants.

Semaj sat there and listened intently, not interrupting or showing any signs of concern. She had a counter offer. One that Raul wasn't going to be able to pass up.

"You know Raul, you should really stop underestimating me," Semaj said, getting up from the bed, and walking over and standing next to the TV. "See, I know all about you. It took me a little time to figure it out, but when I did, I realized that you had every reason to wanna kill me."

"What are you talking about?" he asked, shrugging his shoulders like he had no idea where Semaj was going with this.

"I remember a couple of years back when my grandmother threw this Cuban man out of a blimp with a rope tied around his neck," Semaj said, as she walked across the room to where Qua was standing. "She ended up cutting the man's body up and sending it to his family," Semaj continued, looking at Qua like she was just telling him the story. "I think his name was Julio Ordonez or some shit like that."

"Don't disrespect my brother!" Raul snapped, jumping up from his bed.

Qua immediately pointed his gun at Raul and was a couple of seconds away from pulling the trigger until Semaj placed her hand on top of the gun and lowered it. She slowly walked over to where Raul was standing, got right up in his face and looked him in his eyes.

"Your mother, Catalina, is still alive to this day. Your sister Salina, who you sent back to Cuba a week ago, is still alive. Your daughter and your son and your sister's children are still alive, living in Havana peacefully."

"Are you threatening my family?" Raul questioned, balling up his fist.

"No Raul. I'm making you a promise. If my cousin is not back here within twenty-four hours alive, before I kill you, anybody in this world I think you have so much as a drop of love for will die, and you will be alive to know that their blood is on your hands. So do you want to make the call now and let your mother know to start saying her final prayer? Because she'll be the first to die," Semaj stated without hesitation, and then leaned over, grabbing his cell phone off the bed and passing it to him.

Raul stared at Semaj with pure detest in his eyes.

He had visions of taking a knife and cutting her eyeballs out running through his mind. Every inch of his soul wanted her dead, but he was beginning to accept that was highly unlikely. Instead, he had to focus on saving the life of his family, and the only way that he would be able to make that happen was by placing the call. He stuck his hand down to grab the phone, all the while not breaking eye contact with Semaj. He could see the weakness she once had no longer existed, but what he didn't know was that he was the sole reason for her renewed strength.

$\mathscr{Chapter}$ 19

Over two hundred of Semaj's men participated in the search and rescue for Sosa. Gonzalez and his men stormed the jungle where Raul directed them. No gun battle erupted because the rebels were given strict orders to stand down and allow for Sosa to be released. By the time that Gonzalez got to the tent where Sosa was, he honestly thought that they were too late. She looked as though she was dead. Her face was covered with blood and so was her shirt. She was also naked from the waist down. Gonzalez could see scratches and bruises all over her legs leading to her inner thighs.

Gonzalez kneeled down next to her and checked for a pulse to see if she was alive. The pulse was very light but she had one. From the way her body was beat up there was no doubt in his mind that Sosa had been raped.

"What happened to her?" Gonzalez screamed out at one of the rebels who was at the front entrance of the tent with a cigarette in his mouth.

He had a devious grin on his face looking down at the battered body of Sosa. He was the same rebel who tried to rape her the first time. He had made it his business to finish the job that he'd started, and when Sosa nodded off and took a quick nap, he had come into the tent and beat her until she was unconscious. He had raped her over and over again until he had enough and then he allowed a few other fellow rebels to have their way with her. Every time Sosa woke up, a different man was on top of her ramming his dick inside. When she tried to fight them off, she was knocked right back out.

Gonzalez scooped Sosa up in his arms, took her out of the tent and placed her in his Hummer. The rebel looked on and kept the same grin on his face the whole time.

"Hold on for a minute," Gonzalez said to the medic that had come with him. He walked back over to the tent where the rebel was standing. "You did this, big man?" he asked, standing so close the tip of their noses almost touched.

The rebel chuckled, taking another pull of the cigarette and then blowing the smoke in Gonzalez's face. Gonzalez immediately pulled his .44 magnum from his holster and put it to the rebel's forehead.

"You can't shoot me," the rebel reminded Gonzalez.

Semaj had agreed not to open fire upon any of the rebels as long as they didn't fire on her men. That was the reason why the rebels stood down and let the men onto their land without a fight. Gonzalez was at the point where he didn't care about the treaty. He hated men like the rebel who raped women and starved children. Gonzalez cocked the hammer back on the revolver. The rebel still thought that he was bluffing and decided to take another pull of the cigarette and blow it in Gonzalez's face.

Before all of the smoke had exited the rebel's lungs, Gonzalez pulled the trigger, blowing a chunk of the rebel's head onto the tent. The impact from the bullet crashing through his head splattered blood onto Gonzalez's face and he could literally taste the gunpowder from the blast in his mouth.

None of the other rebels did anything, mainly because they were outnumbered and didn't stand a chance of making it through the gun battle. They watched as Gonzalez wiped the blood off his face and headed back to his truck. A loud whistle from Gonzalez and a twirl of his finger prompted all of his men to rally up and head back home.

Due to a new chain of events, Semaj postponed the Tent meeting until tomorrow. All of the members had agreed to it without question, especially since Semaj said that she had the person responsible for trying to kill her in custody. Everyone was curious to know who it was, all except for the people that were involved. This was an unsettling situation that needed to be dealt with before all of the families could get back to conducting business. The Espreilla Family was too important to the Tent, so this issue required everyone's undivided attention.

Until Semaj knew that Sosa was alive and safe, she, Qua, and Raul made themselves real comfortable in the hotel room. Raul knew that once Sosa was found Semaj was going to kill him, but before she did that he had one last trick up his sleeve. Semaj looked down at her phone on the table as it began to vibrate, breaking the silence in the room. She could see that it was Gonzalez calling. She feared answering it, thinking that he was going to be delivering some bad news, like Sosa being dead or them not finding her at all. She was well aware of how vicious the cartel could be and what they were capable of doing. Not even somebody like Raul could guarantee that Sosa would make it out of the jungle alive.

"Hello," Semaj answered, looking out of the hotel room window.

"We have Sosa. She's in bad shape, but she is alive," Gonzalez reported.

"What do you mean bad shape? Is she going to make it?" Semaj asked, looking over at Raul.

"Your cousin is tough as nails. I know she is going to make a full recovery," Gonzalez said, as he looked down while doctors worked on her.

On that note, Semaj hung up the phone and then walked over to the bed where Raul was sitting. She pulled the Glock 9mm from her front pocket and screwed the silencer on to it.

"You know your assassination doesn't stop with me," Raul said, lifting his head up to look at Semaj. "They won't stop until you are dead."

"And who is they?" Semaj asked, cocking a bullet into the chamber.

"There is somebody else in the Tent that wants you dead. Do you honestly think that I was acting alone on this?" Raul said, folding his arms across his chest. "They tried to kill me this morning because I couldn't get the job done but I ended up killing the person that they sent to my hotel room."

Semaj stood there and listened to Raul talk. She couldn't believe what her ears were hearing. This shit was bigger than Raul, even though he had somewhat of a legitimate reason for wanting her dead.

"So who is it?" Semaj asked, again.

"Oh no, Semaj. If I tell you that, you'll still put a bullet in my head. I gave you Sosa so you wouldn't hurt my family, and now I am trying to preserve my own life," Raul conceded.

The room became silent once again. Semaj really had to contemplate whether his information was worth allowing him to live. Whoever else in the Tent wanted her dead needed to be stopped by way of a bullet, and the only person who had the information was Raul.

"I see it like this. You let me live and I'll tell you who it is. I'll give you my word that I will never come after you again and I will give up my chair at the table. For the death of my brother, you can say that we are even for everything I put you and your cousin through," Raul offered.

Semaj took a step back and looked over at Qua,

who wasn't enthused about his offer. "I know you ain't considering that bullshit," Qua said, leaning off the wall and walking over to Semaj.

Semaj grabbed Qua's arm and led him into the bathroom where they could talk in privacy. Raul thought about jumping up and making a break for the door, but had second thoughts once he saw that the bathroom door wasn't closed all the way. He wouldn't have made it to the door if he tried.

"Maj, don't play around wit this dude. I think we should kill him and get it over with. If you want, we can kill every last one of these mafuckas in the Tent," Qua reasoned.

Semaj smiled, thinking of how much Qua reminded her of her dad. But just like she told Mitch, it was bigger than that and everybody in the Tent shouldn't have to suffer for one or two people. Besides, killing all of the members of the 16 Tent was damn near impossible. They weren't sweet by a long shot and Semaj didn't have enough energy and manpower to war with some of the most violent people in the world.

"Qua, I need you to trust me on this one. It's gonna be like killing two birds with one stone," Semaj said, looking out the bathroom door at Raul. "If my plan doesn't work we'll consider your idea. But first I have to at least try to save this organization."

Qua sat there with an angry look on his face, but he really had no other choice but to ride with Semaj. He put his hand on top of her shoulder and pulled Semaj closer to him. "Be careful Maj. Whatever you wanna do I am here for you, just be careful. A'ight Ma?" he said, looking down at her.

Semaj nodded her head in agreement, wrapping her arms around his waist. She looked up at him and was so caught up in the moment she leaned in for a kiss. Her lips pressed up against Qua's, and for a minute, it felt like he had lifted her off of her feet. The inside of his mouth tasted like he'd just finished eating a piece of cherry candy and the scent from his cologne almost had Semaj feeling some sort of a sexual euphoria.

"Hmmm!" Semaj moaned pushing away from him.

She swung the bathroom door open and headed back into the room with Raul. Qua stayed back in order to let his rock hard dick go down. Semaj walked right up to Raul with her gun still in her hand. "You have a deal. Now talk." Semaj said, unscrewing the silencer and tucking the gun away.

Raul looked at her with a smile. "Nikolai sure has a thing for you."

Nikolai sat in the hotel room throwing back the little shot bottles from the mini bar. The head of her security was with her trying to convince her that she should leave instead of attending the meeting tomorrow. He probably was the only person in her camp that knew what was going on. Nikolai being as stubborn as she was wouldn't allow herself to leave. She wanted to see how everything was going to play out. Running wasn't an option. Before she did that, she would do her best to eliminate any potential threats that could expose her. The only threat that she saw relevant enough to confront was Raul. Not only could he pull her into it but he also knew Nikolai or Marko tried to have him killed. He definitely was the target but the hotel had so much security in it, it was virtually impossible to get at him as long as he stayed there. Hell, Nikolai didn't even know which room he had checked into earlier that day. All she knew is that Semaj wanted everybody to stay at this hotel for the night.

"There has to be a way for us to get to Raul," Nikolai told Ethan, the head of her security, while he massaged her feet. "He doesn't even have guards with him."

"True, but all of the other members do and their security is just as good as being his," Ethan said, rubbing the oil in between her toes.

It was a complicated situation that needed a great deal of thought. Nikolai pulled her foot from out of Ethan's hand and then sat back on the bed. She grabbed one of her cigarettes off the nightstand and lit it.

"Come help me think," she said, sliding her nightgown over her waist.

She snapped her finger and tapped on the side of her thigh as she spread her limbs apart. Ethan did what he was told like a dog listening to the commands of his owner. Without another word being said, he climbed on top of the bed, laid flat on his stomach, placed his face into Nikolai's pussy, and began licking it. This was like a form of mental therapy for Nikolai. Some people like to meditate, and others like to indulge in other kinds of activities, but Nikolai liked to get her pussy licked by men young enough to be her son. Some of her greatest ideas popped up in her head while she was getting oral sex. If Ethan licked her clit as good as she needed him to, somebody was definitely going to get shot tomorrow.

Sosa cracked her eye open to see a nurse standing beside her checking the IV in her arm. Her other eye was swollen shut so it was kind of hard for her to see. For a moment, she actually thought she was dreaming because there was no way she could still be alive after everything she had endured. The nurse looked down just in time to see Sosa's one eye open before she closed it again.

Sosa was exhausted and her entire body was in pain from the brutal assault. She'd lost a nice amount of blood and was dehydrated from the attack. One of her rib bones was broken and her eye socket sustained some damage. Aside from all of that and the expected mental damage she would have from the rape, Sosa was recovering well. Her vitals were good and she began to go in and out of consciousness every 15 to 20 minutes. She still had a long way to go but doctors were sure that she would make a full recovery.

Chapter 20

Qua stayed up all night long, watching Raul with a sharp eye. Raul stayed up all night too, but only faked as if he was asleep just in case the opportunity presented itself to get up and creep out of the room. Qua didn't fall for it though. He was too smart to get caught slipping. Semaj on the other hand slept pretty good in the king-sized bed. She could do that because she knew beyond a shadow of a doubt that she was well-protected with Qua by her side.

"Yo Maj," Qua said, tapping her shoulder.

She opened her eyes to see Qua sitting beside her. A smile came over her face thinking about how she used to love waking up next to him. "Come on, get up," he said, tapping her lightly on her hip and then getting up from the bed himself.

Semaj sat up on the bed, looking over at the clock on the nightstand. The morning had come fast as hell. It was already 8:00 and the meeting was scheduled for 9:00. She watched as Qua walked over and kicked the side of the couch to wake up Raul, who had only really fallen asleep about an hour ago.

"Go ahead and get in the shower. You got about a half hour before we start making our way downstairs," Qua told Semaj as he checked his gun, and the extra ammunition he got Ron to bring to him last night.

Semaj's security consisted of Qua, Murder Mitch, Penny, and the two guards that came with Vikingo. She was more on some hood shit than anything at this point and the only people she felt comfortable with standing behind her were family. She hopped out of the bed, grabbed her luggage and headed for the bathroom. Today was going to be a big day and it might determine how long Semaj would sit on her throne. Either way, she was ready to confront the situation head on.

All kinds of guns were being loaded and cocked in Marco's room, and in the two rooms across the hall where his security stayed. He knew that there was no way any of the attempts on Semaj's life could come back on him, but just in case things did get ugly and took an unexpected turn, he was going to make sure he was well-equipped to make an exit out of the building.

He stood in the middle of his hotel room smoking on a cigar, listening and watching his men prepare themselves as if they were about to go to war. He could never get enough of how organized his men were and how mob-like they dressed in suits. He had a crew of stone cold killers with him and every last one of them were trained pros.

"Yo, let me speak to you for a minute," Qua said, walking into the bathroom as Semaj was looking in the mirror.

He closed the door just enough so that he could still see Raul sitting on the couch. He walked up and stood right behind Semaj as she pulled her hair into a ponytail. He couldn't help but grab her by the waist and pull her closer to him. She was fully dressed in a cream linen suit but Qua could still feel the softness of her ass pressed up against his dick.

"You know I love you, right?" he said, resting his chin on Semaj's shoulder.

Feeling him so close to her always did something to Semaj. She leaned her head back, grabbed his hands, and wrapped his arms around her stomach.

"What are you doin' Qua?" she said, looking at their reflection in the mirror.

"Maj, I need you," he confessed, looking at her through the mirror. "You don't know how much I love you."

"Yes I do, because I love you just as much." Semaj turned around to face him. "But we can't...I can't..."

"I'm empty without you. I swear my heart won't allow me to love anybody else no matter how hard I try, and I don't wanna go on the rest of my life without having you in it," he said, looking her in her eyes.

As hard as it was to admit, Semaj understood exactly how he felt, because deep down inside she felt the same way about him. She loved Qua, and that was something that could never change. Even though Vikingo had managed to earn some of that love, he would never be able to possess all of it.

"Do you know how much I want to say 'fuck it' and be with you and only you? But things are much more complicated. Vikingo needs me and I can't just up and leave him like that," she said, resting her forehead against his chest, feeling torn.

"Maj, look at me," he said, lifting her chin up. "Please don't make me beg you," he said, as his eyes began to fill up with tears.

Semaj had never seen this side of Qua before. He rarely showed his emotions, but he wanted his woman back and it didn't matter the cost. He felt like he'd lived long enough without her and he was going to stop at nothing to try to get her back, even if that meant showing his vulnerable side. His willingness to open his heart and share his feelings had Semaj tearing up herself.

"Oh my God," she mumbled, wiping the tears from her eyes. Please, Qua, can you give me some time? I'm not saying no. I just need time to figure some things out," she pleaded.

They both sat there and held each other for a moment. It wasn't until Qua looked down at his watch and saw that it was 10 minutes until 9:00 that he remembered about the Tent meeting. He looked through the crack in the door to see Raul still sitting there on the couch.

"Yo, you ready for this?" Qua asked, lifting her chin up so that he could look into her eyes. She nodded her head yes and then turned around to look at herself in the mirror.

"Just give me two minutes and I will be right out," she told Qua, in order to freshen up her face from crying.

As he was walking out the door Semaj stopped him. "I love you Qua," she said, and then turned back around to finish washing her face.

Nikolai stood in her room looking out of the window at the city while smoking a cigarette. She could hear her room door open but did not take her eyes off of the view. "It's time," Ethan said, as he walked up behind her. Nikolai didn't say a word. She took another pull of the cigarette, batted it out in the ashtray and then turned to face Ethan. She smiled at him, reached over and tapped the side of his face twice, then pointed towards the door for him to lead the way.

Today should be interesting," Ezra told his wife as he stopped at the door before leaving the room.

She stood there reaching up and readjusting his tie. She had a concerned look on her face that Ezra could not ignore. "What's wrong Umma?" he asked his wife, wondering what she was thinking.

She looked at him not wanting to say what she was thinking, but Ezra knew his wife better than she knew herself. He thought that it was kind of funny that Umma may have thought he had something to do with the assassination attempt on Semaj.

"What?" I didn't have anything to do with this," Ezra chuckled, shaking his head.

Umma playfully grabbed him by the tie and tried to pull him down to her, but Ezra resisted, wrapping his arms around her waist and lifting her into the air. Behind closed doors, they were playful like that, but even though it seemed like a joking matter, Umma was kind of relieved that Ezra didn't have anything to do with what was going on with Semaj. She, along with everybody else, knew the outcome for the person responsible for violating the Tent's legislation.

"I love you Ezra," Umma said, as he held her in the air and up against his chest. "You know that, don't you?"

"Yes, my queen. I know," he answered, pressing his lips against hers. "Now, let's go see who's head will be on the chopping block," he said, putting Umma down and extending his hand out in front of her. Umma reached behind her back and pulled two twin, chrome .50 caliber Desert Eagles out, passing one of them to him. She cocked the other one back slightly to make sure that she had put a bullet in the chamber. Ezra did the same thing before stuffing the gun into his front waistband. When he opened his hotel room door, four tall black, muscular men from his security team were standing there waiting to escort Ezra and his wife to the ballroom.

Wong Won threw back two shots of scotch sitting at the table in his hotel room. He knew that more than likely he was going to need them for what was about to take place. He had a gut feeling that something bad was about to happen but it wasn't in his nature to tuck his tail and go the opposite way. In fact, Wong Won liked drama and was going to be the first person to volunteer to issue the possible death sentence to whoever was found guilty for trying to kill a Tent member.

He looked down at his watch and then stood up and brushed the lint off of his suit. His three security guards rose to their feet as well without Won having to say a word. There was no need for his men to get ready, nor did he have to give them a pep talk. They were few in number but possibly the most deadly out of everybody's security.

Wong Won adjusted the black .45 Mil automatic on his waist, buttoned up his blazer to conceal it and then headed for the door. His men were right behind him looking like they were Chinese Secret service members protecting their president.

Semaj came out of the bathroom looking a little more refreshed. Qua was waiting outside the door with her Glock 9mm, passing it to her along with an extra clip. A knock at the door grabbed everybody's attention, but

Qua already knew who it was. He opened the door and stepped to the side so that Murda Mitch and Penny could enter the room. Two of Semaj's Colombian guards, Julio and Tito, stood in the hallway instead of coming into the room.

Murda Mitch definitely was on some hood shit. He had on a black hoodie, black jeans, a pair of 3.25 tan Timberland boots, and he didn't have a lick of jewelry on. His hands were wrapped around two 10 millimeters inside of his hoodie pockets and he had a look on his face like he wasn't playing any games today.

Penny looked hood too. She had on some black jeans, a cream thermal with a black t-shirt on top of it and a pair of black and white Jordan's. In her right back pocket was a black with a gray slide .45 automatic and in her left back pocket were two extra clips, one of which was extended. Even Raul couldn't deny that Semaj's team appeared gutter, but in a good way. Everybody seemed focused.

"Let's get this shit over wit'," Mitch said, pulling the two 10 millimeters out to check and make sure that he had bullets in the chambers.

The only way Semaj could get permission to kill Nikolai was if Raul testified before all of the members of the Tent. He even had a key piece of evidence to corroborate his story. He just wasn't going to give it up until he knew that his life would be spared. Being as though the attack was against Semaj, more than likely the members would probably leave his fate up to her. What

Raul had was well worth allowing him to live. He had a recorded conversation with him and Nikolai speaking about the plot to kill Semaj in detail and for what reasons.

He had recorded the conversation for insurance purposes just like he did with Sosa. He was the only person who could access the conversation by way of his cell phone; it was saved in his messages and he was the only person with the four-digit code. Without the recorded conversation between Nikolai and Raul, it would be his word against hers, making it much more difficult for the members to believe him over Nikolai. Especially since she had way more time in as a Tent member than Raul. It would be hard for the majority of the members to rule in Semaj's favor, which could potentially cause problems between the families.

Bottom line, Raul was all Semaj had to present to the families to state her cause for action, so from this point on he was considered precious cargo.

"Let's roll out," Semaj said, heading towards the door.

Qua walked over to the couch where Raul was sitting and motioned for him to get up and start walking. Qua and Murda Mitch were behind him, and once in the hallway, Semaj directed the two guards to stay in front of him. Penny walked alongside Semaj. They all headed down the hallway until they made it to small lobby where the two elevators were. Everybody stopped and waited for Semaj's instructions.

She looked around for a second, not wanting to

split up, but at the same time not thinking it was the best idea to have everybody packed on the elevator.

"You and you, come with me," Semaj said, pointing to Qua and one of her guards. "We're taking Raul with us. Mitch, take Penny and Tito with you and meet me on the 1st floor," she directed as she pushed the elevator button on the side of the wall.

It took a couple of minutes for Semaj's elevator to reach the floor. Mitch looked on as Semaj, Qua, Raul, and Julio got onto the elevator, and at the exact moment that the doors were closing, and overwhelmingly bad feeling came over him.

"Maj!" Mitch called out right before the doors closed.

Semaj had already hit the 1st floor button, so the elevator began to move immediately once the doors closed. It didn't go far because someone had pushed the elevator button for the 23rd floor right below them, which caused the elevator to stop. When the doors opened, they were expecting for somebody to be there but no one was there. Semaj tapped the close button on the panel so they could continue moving.

The same thing happened when the elevator stopped on the 21st floor. The doors opened but there was nobody there. Then it was the 20th, 19th, 18th, and the 17th, still nobody was waiting. Semaj got out of the elevator on the 17th floor to look around the hallway.

"You good?" Qua asked, standing in between the doors.

"Yeah it's probably some bad ass kids playing around, she said, walking back to the elevator.

Out of anger, she smacked the 1st floor button three or four times and then put her back up against the wall. The doors closed and the elevator began to move again, but only to stop on the next floor below. Semaj looked up at the ceiling in frustration. Raul was probably the only person on the elevator who had a feeling their car stopped at every floor for a reason. Before the doors even opened, he inched his way a little to the right so that he was standing directly behind Julio in the middle of the car. Semaj and Qua had their backs against the wall on opposite sides of the car looking at each other.

As the elevator door opened there was an image of a man standing there and in his hand was a large .357 automatic with an extended clip and a silencer screwed onto it. Julio didn't even have a chance to react. He took the first bullet in the center of his chest, knocking him backwards onto Raul. Qua and Semaj's reaction time was swift, as both of them moved up to the front of the car behind the small wall to get out of the direct line of fire.

The gunman continued to fire into the elevator, gunning for his main target, Raul. Raul tried to hold Julio up as a shield, which worked for a split second as he took two more bullets to his chest and head, but the bullets kept coming and the shooter wasn't letting up. Neither Qua or Semaj could compose themselves long enough to draw their weapons. They were more focused on avoiding the hot lead balls being fired in their direction.

Semaj reached down and pushed any and every button she could get her fingers on so that the elevator door would close. As it started to, the shooter walked up a little closer and fired his last few rounds into the elevator right before the doors shut. His aim was more accurate this time, striking Raul once in his neck and again directly in his left eye. His body slumped over onto Julio in the middle of the elevator, right in front of Semaj's face.

"Maj, you good?" Qua yelled out as the elevator came to a stop on the next floor.

"Yeah, I'm good."

Qua pulled his gun immediately, not knowing if another gunman was going to open fire once the doors opened again. Semaj stood there in a daze, looking down at her only chance of proving Nikolai had something to do with the attempts on her life. Without him, she didn't have anything else to go off of except for his word and that wasn't going to be able to hold water in the Tent meeting, especially now that he was dead.

"Come on," Qua said, when the doors opened, grabbing Semaj by the arm and pulling her out of the elevator.

Semaj followed, but right before the doors closed, she remembered Raul's cell phone and the important contents that it held. "Hold up, I have to get his phone," she said, pulling away from Qua as she caught the doors right before they closed. She went in and searched through his pockets until she found it.

"You got it?" Qua asked, as she was coming out of

the elevator.

"Yeah, I got it," she answered, looking at the phone and then putting it into her pocket.

"A'ight, let's get the fuck out of here," he said, grabbing her hand.

'Wait." Semaj didn't budge. The elevator door had closed and was on its way to the next floor, but she just stood there.

"Come on! We need to find Mitch and them and get the fuck outta here!"

"And go where, Qua?" she snapped, putting her hand on her hip.

"After we get our people, I don't care where we go, but we gotta get the fuck outta this hotel. There are two dead bodies in that elevator. This place is about to be swarming with cops."

"I'm not leaving."

"What the fuck is wrong wit' you?" Qua yelled, flinging his arms up in frustration before bringing them back down.

"They tried to kill me and I'm not going anywhere until I finish what I came here for," Semaj screamed back.

Qua didn't know what else he could say or do. Semaj was on a mission and she was determined to see it through even if it killed her.

"So what you wanna do, 'cause we in this together? But we need to decide quick 'cause the cops will be here any minute."

Semaj looked at Qua and then over at the door that

led to the stairwell. "I don't know about you, Qua, but I got a meeting to attend," she said in a calm voice.

"Like I told you Semaj, we in this together...so lets go," Qua said, before pushing the door open. "Lead the way."

To Be Continued.....

Coming Soon...The
Final Installment

MAFIA

Princess

PART 5...The
Takeover

A KING PRODUCTION

Dior Comes Home..

Rich
or
Famous
Part 2

JOY DEJA KING

Prologue

Lorenzo stepped out of his black Bugatti Coupe and entered the non-descript building in East Harlem. Normally, Lorenzo would have at least one henchman with him, but he wanted complete anonymity. When he made his entrance, the man Lorenzo planned on hiring was patiently waiting.

"I hope you came prepared for what I need."

"I wouldn't have wasted my time if I hadn't," Lorenzo stated before pulling out two pictures from a manila envelope and tossing them on the table.

"This is her?"

"Yes, her name is Alexus. Study this face very carefully, 'cause this is the woman you're going to bring to me, so I can kill."

"Are you sure you don't want me to handle it? Murder is included in my fee."

"I know, but personally killing this backstabbing snake is a gift to myself"

"Who is the other woman?"

"Her name is Lala."

"Do you want her dead, too?"

"I haven't decided. For now, just find her whereabouts and any other pertinent information. She also has a young daughter. I want you to find out how the little girl is doing. That will determine whether Lala lives or dies."

"Is there anybody else on your hit list?"

"This is it for now, but that might change at any moment. Now, get on your job, because I want results ASAP," Lorenzo demanded before tossing stacks of money next to the photos.

"I don't think there's a need to count. I'm sure it's all there," the hit man said, picking up one of the stacks and flipping through the bills.

"No doubt, and you can make even more, depending on how quickly I see results."

"I appreciate the extra incentive."

"It's not for you, it's for me. Everyone that is responsible for me losing the love of my life will pay in blood. The sooner the better."

Lorenzo didn't say another word and instead made his exit. He came and delivered; the rest was up to the hit man he had hired. But Lorenzo wasn't worried, he was just one of the many killers on his payroll hired to do the exact same job. He wanted to guarantee that Alexus was delivered to him alive. In his heart, he not only blamed Alexus and Lala for getting him locked up, but also held both of them responsible for Dior taking her own life. As he sat in his jail cell, Lorenzo promised himself that once he got out, if need be he would spend the rest of his life making sure both women received the ultimate retribution.

A KING PRODUCTION

I'm Gettin' That Helicopter Money...

Bad Bitch

JOY DEJA KING

"He need a Bad Bitch help him wit' cash flow.
I'm his Boss Bitch find me at his trap door.
I'm his type I'm what he asked for.
My nigga gettin' money,
I say get some more…"

Joy Deja King—Bad Bitch

Aaliyah

I came into the world surrounded by wealth and privilege. I could've been anything I wanted to be and I was...I was a Bad Bitch on my way to gettin' that helicopter money and I was loving every minute of it. I chose to walk on the same path as my Grandfather and Father but in different shoes. As I thought about my Grandfather, someone I respected and loved more than just about anybody else in this world, there was one thing I would do differently than him. If I had my way, Maya would've been dead by now, but there was no doubt in my mind that I would accomplish the very thing no one had been able to do, including my Mother. I would make sure Maya took her last breath and was six feet under, sooner rather than later.

I stood in front of the arched window, soaking in the breathtaking views of downtown Miami's skyline from over 250 feet of open bay frontage. Watching as the wind ushered the waves towards the shore, with the sun's golden light shining on the rippling water was the closest I had gotten to serenity in what seemed like many years. My life had me on a nonstop ride of one disaster after another. Starting with being accused of Sway's murder and then sitting in jail until I stood trial. Then my Grandfather being shot and in a coma, my parent's getting separated to breaking up with Amir which was still taking a toll on me emotionally after all these months. So many things in my life had changed, but so many other things stayed the same.

"Are you ready to go?"

"Dale, you startled me," I gasped, when I heard his voice. I turned around and he was standing in the door entrance.

"I apologize. Wherever your mind was, it had to be in deep thought."

"I guess you could say that."

"Is it anything you want to talk about?"

"No, I'm good."

"You sure? You know you can talk to me about anything. Remember you're my protégé. It's in my best interest to always make sure nothing is keeping you from being at the top of your game."

"I understand that but there's no need to worry. I won't disappoint you or myself. I'm in this game to win and I won't accept anything less than that."

"Then I take it you're ready for our meeting so lets go."

"Of course I am," I grinned, grabbing my purse off the living room table.

We headed outside towards the awaiting car and like always I looked up at the towering palm trees and a smile crept across my face. Miami had become a place that I treasured because everything about it gave me something that New York/New Jersey never could and that was peace.

"Do you feel prepared for the meeting?" Dale questioned, once again taking me away from my private thoughts. I knew he meant well but I was looking forward to having some much needed time alone.

"Yes. We've already gone over this. You're going to lead the conversation. I'm going to sit and listen and when you're ready for me to give additional critical information, you'll casually lean forward and that will be my cue to step in," I stated with an underlying annoyance in my tone.

"No need to get irritated," Dale said, placing his hand on my upper left thigh. "You don't seem quite yourself today so you can't blame me for being concerned. You know how important this meeting is."

"I get that, but have I ever dropped the ball on anything that has to do with business?"

"No and I wanna make sure you keep it that way."

I turned and gazed out the backseat window as the driver made his way to Indian Creek Island for our meeting. I didn't respond to what Dale said because I couldn't deny that I was "off" today. As much stress as the East Coast brought me it was home and I missed my family and more importantly my heart ached for Amir.

"Is it Maya, is that what has your mind someplace else?"

I simply nodded my head yes. I figured that sounded much better than having to confess to Dale I was yearning for my ex.

"I already told you when the time was right Maya would be handled. You need to let that go for now. We have much bigger and significant deals on the table right now that have to be dealt with."

"You're right. I just don't want Maya to slip away. She's been a thorn in my family's lives for far too long and the Peaches situation was the final nail in her coffin. Even the thought of her slipping through my fingers, burns me up inside."

"That's not gonna happen. I got my people keeping track of all her movements. Like I promised you, when the time is right, I will bring Maya to you and you can personally take pleasure in ending her life once and for all. You have to believe that."

"I do. I do believe that," I nodded, looking back out the window. I had learned never to doubt Dale's word. Each thing that he promised me thus far, he delivered it and more. Proof of that was being shown to me once again, as the driver made his way up the long elegant landscaped driveway at 12 Indian Creek Drive. This home was located on Dade County's most prestigious Private Island. I'm talking homes that start at 30 million and go nowhere but up. Juan Alvarez, the head of one of the most profitable and deadliest Mexican Cartels, owned the palatial estate we were now entering. This was the man that would take me to making that helicopter money, purchasing private jets, buying islands and shit like that.

After our ordeal with Peaches and I had to murder that bitch, I became completed fixated on two things: Killing Maya and making money. Dale promised that he would make sure I achieved both. When I realized Maya had set me up to be killed, she was at the top of my list to fall. Dale convinced me to hold back and let that shit settle for a while. At first I resisted his suggestion but I had watched Dale and I respected how he moved in handling his business so I listened to his logic and followed it. He told me to focus my energy on stacking paper because the money would give me all the power I needed, to eliminate Maya and just about anybody else I felt was a threat to me or my family.

After several months of soaking up any and every business move Dale and his brother Emory made, I became the female version of them which made me all the more lethal. I became meticulous with how I handled money, drugs and people we did business with and the more moves I made I wanted to make even bigger ones. Because men dominated the drug business, I had no problem using the female persuasion to my advantage. I dangled it just enough to keep my creditability intact but to also allow our business associates to lower their wall enough for me to get the information I needed to close better deals. It was that calculated maneuvering that put the name Juan Alvarez on my radar. Everyone including

Emory swore it would be impossible to get to him. The only person that didn't flinch was Dale. Like me he loved a challenge and like he promised, against all the odds here we were.

When we pulled through the iron gates in every direction you turned there appeared to be armed guards. He had an army watching over him like he was the President of the United States but in the world of drugs I guess you could say Juan Alvarez was.

"This place is unbelievable," I commented, as we got closer to his massive mansion. I had lived and seen many stunning homes in my short lifetime but this place was something completely different. The sprawling European design was beyond breathtaking.

"That it is. But if we play our cards right we'll be able to have one just like it," Dale stated, with unwavering confidence. I couldn't help but smile because like always he made me a believer.

In the brief moment from me glancing over at Dale and smiling at his comment, before our driver could even step out and open the door for us, there was an armed guard on both sides of the car doing that job for him. They immediately began patting us down and I looked over at Dale and he nodded his head letting me know to go with the flow. I planned on doing that anyway. We had come this far I wasn't about to fuck it up now.

"Follow us," the guard that had just finished patting Dale down said, directing us towards the front entrance. A 40 ft. hand-painted ceiling with gold leaf accents in the foyer greeted us. I wanted to gasp as we walked through what had to be over 40,000 square ft. of what I would describe as a grand and majestic masterpiece. After what felt like a never-ending marathon we finally ended up outside. Off in the distance I noticed the dock with a huge yacht and a private lagoon. But it was the over 50-foot long mosaic tiled 24k gold lined pool that truly had me in awe. The water seemed to be calling my name but that feeling didn't last long because once again there were armed guards posted everywhere. Seeing them took all sense of peace or relaxation away but I assumed that was the purpose they were there to serve.

"Mr. Alvarez, your guest have arrived," the guard that had led us in announced. I still couldn't see him because he was sitting down on a high gloss white circular sofa with his back turned to us. I noticed him signaling the guard by putting up one finger. "He's on a call. He'll be with you both shortly," the guard informed us.

I appreciated having a little extra time before we were formally introduced because out of nowhere a burst of nervousness crept up on me. That was so not my style as Dale had taught me how to remain calm even under the most strenuous situations. He warned me that keeping a composed demeanor could be the difference between living and dying in certain predicaments. I quickly closed my eyes and let out a soft breath to center myself and regain control. In that instant I realized where all the anxiety was coming from. I was about to meet the man that would change my life forever.

A King Production presents…

A Novel

JOY DEJA KING

Power

NO ONE MAN SHOULD HAVE ALL THAT POWER...BUT THERE WERE TWO

JOY DEJA KING

Chapter 1

Underground King

Alex stepped into his attorney's office to discuss what was always his number one priority...business. When he sat down their eyes locked and there was complete silence for the first few seconds. This was Alex's way of setting the tone of the meeting. His silence spoke volumes. This might've been his attorney's office but he was the head nigga in charge and nothing got started until he decided it was time to speak. Alex felt this approach was necessary. You see, after all these years of them doing business, attorney George Lofton still wasn't used to dealing with a man like Alex; a dirt-poor kid who could've easily died in the projects he was born in, but instead made millions. It wasn't done the ski mask way but it was still illegal.

They'd first met when Alex was a sixteen-year-old kid growing up in TechWood Homes, a housing project in Atlanta. Alex and his best friend, Deion, had been arrested because the principal found 32 crack vials in

Alex's book bag. Another kid had tipped the principal off and the principal subsequently called the police. Alex and Deion were arrested and suspended from school. His mother called George, who had the charges against them dismissed and they were allowed to go back to school. But that wasn't the last time he would use George. He was arrested at twenty-two for attempted murder and for trafficking cocaine a year later. Alex was acquitted on both charges. George Lofton later became known as the best trial attorney in Atlanta, but Alex had also become the best at what he did. And since it was Alex's money that kept Mr. Lofton in designer suits, million dollar homes and foreign cars, he believed he called the shots, and dared his attorney to tell him differently.

Alex noticed that what seemed like a long period of silence made Mr. Lofton feel uncomfortable, which he liked. Out of habit, in order to camouflage the discomfort, his attorney always kept bottled water within arm's reach. He would cough then take a swig, lean back in his chair, raise his eyebrows a little, trying to give a look of certainty, though he wasn't completely confident at all in Alex's presence. The reason was because Alex did what many had thought would be impossible, especially men like George Lofton. He had gone from a knucklehead, low-level drug dealer to an underground king and an unstoppable respected criminal boss.

Before finally speaking, Alex gave an intense stare into George Lofton's piercing eyes. They were not only the bluest he had ever seen, but also some of the most calculating. The latter is what Alex found so compelling. A calculating attorney working on his behalf could almost guarantee a get out of jail card for the duration of his criminal career.

"Have you thought over what we briefly discussed the other day?" Alex asked his attorney, finally breaking the silence.

"Yes I have, but I want to make sure I understand you correctly. You want to give me six hundred thousand to represent you or your friend Deion if you are ever arrested and have to stand trial again in the future?"

Alex assumed he had already made himself clear based on their previous conversations and was annoyed by what he now considered a repetitive question. "George, you know I don't like repeating myself. That's exactly what I'm saying. Are we clear?"

"So this is an unofficial retainer."

"Yes, you can call it that."

George stood and closed the blinds then walked over to the door that led to the reception area. He turned the deadbolt so they wouldn't be disturbed. George sat back behind the desk. "You know that if you and your friend Deion are ever on the same case that I can't represent the both of you."

"I know that."

"So what do you propose I do if that was ever to happen?"

"You would get him the next best attorney in Atlanta," Alex said without hesitation. Deion was Alex's best friend—had been since the first grade. They were now business partners, but the core of their bond was built on that friendship, and because of that Alex would always look out for Deion's best interest.

"That's all I need to know."

Alex clasped his hands and stared at the ceiling for a moment thinking that maybe it was a bad idea bringing the money to George. Maybe he should have just put it somewhere safe only known to him and his mom. He quickly dismissed his concerns.

"Okay. Where's the money?" Alex presented him with two leather briefcases. George opened the first one and was glad to see that it was all hundred-dollar bills. When he closed the briefcase he asked, "There is no need to count this is there?"

"You can count it if you want, but it's all there."

George took another swig of water. The cash made him nervous. He planned to take it directly to one of his bank safe deposit boxes. The two men stood. Alex was a foot taller than George; he had flawless mahogany skin, a deep brown with a bit of a red tint, broad shoulders, very large hands, and a goatee. He was a man's man. With such a powerful physical appearance, Alex kept his style very low-key. His only display of wealth was a pricey diamond watch that his best friend and partner Deion had bought him for his birthday.

"I'll take good care of this, and you," his attorney said, extending his hand to Alex.

"With this type of money, I know you will," Alex

stated without flinching. Alex gave one last lingering stare into his attorney's piercing eyes. "We do have a clear understanding...correct?"

"Of course. I've never let you down and I never will. That, I promise you." The men shook hands and Alex made his exit with the same coolness as his entrance.

With Alex embarking on a new, potentially dangerous business venture, he wanted to make sure that he had all his bases covered. The higher up he seemed to go on the totem pole, the costlier his problems became. But Alex welcomed new challenges because he had no intentions of ever being a nickel and dime nigga again.

A KING PRODUCTION

Baller Bitches

VOLUME 1
PARTS 1-3

A NOVEL

JOY DEJA KING

A KING PRODUCTION

Baller Bitches

VOLUME 2
PARTS 4-6

A NOVEL

JOY DEJA KING

A KING PRODUCTION

Young Diamond Books

PRESENTS

A young adult urban tale

Ride
Wit' Me
2

JOY DEJA KING

Coming Soon!

Genesis & Genevieve...Born Sinners

A King Production
Order Form

A King Production
P.O. Box 912
Collierville, TN 38027
www.joydejaking.com
www.twitter.com/joydejaking

Name: _____
Address: _____
City/State: _____
Zip: _____

QUANTITY	TITLES	PRICE	TOTAL
____	Bitch	$15.00	____
____	Bitch Reloaded	$15.00	____
____	The Bitch Is Back	$15.00	____
____	Queen Bitch	$15.00	____
____	Last Bitch Standing	$15.00	____
____	Superstar	$15.00	____
____	Ride Wit' Me	$12.00	____
____	Stackin' Paper	$15.00	____
____	Trife Life To Lavish	$15.00	____
____	Trife Life To Lavish II	$15.00	____
____	Stackin' Paper II	$15.00	____
____	Rich or Famous	$15.00	____
____	Bitch A New Beginning	$15.00	____
____	Mafia Princess Part 1	$15.00	____
____	Mafia Princess Part 2	$15.00	____
____	Mafia Princess Part 3	$15.00	____
____	Mafia Princess Part 4	$15.00	____
____	Boss Bitch	$15.00	____
____	Baller Bitches Vol. 1	$15.00	____
____	Bad Bitch	$15.00	____
____	Princess Fever "Birthday Bash"	$9.99	____

Shipping/Handling (Via Priority Mail) $6.50 1-2 Books, $8.95 3-4 Books add $1.95 for ea. Additional book.

Total: $_____ FORMS OF ACCEPTED PAYMENTS: Certified or government issued checks and money Orders, all mail in orders take 5-7 Business days to be delivered.

A King Production
Order Form

A King Production
P.O. Box 912
Collierville, TN 38027
www.joydejaking.com
www.twitter.com/joydejaking

Name: _____

Address: _____

City/State: _____

Zip: _____

QUANTITY	TITLES	PRICE	TOTAL
____	Bitch	$15.00	____
____	Bitch Reloaded	$15.00	____
____	The Bitch Is Back	$15.00	____
____	Queen Bitch	$15.00	____
____	Last Bitch Standing	$15.00	____
____	Superstar	$15.00	____
____	Ride Wit' Me	$12.00	____
____	Stackin' Paper	$15.00	____
____	Trife Life To Lavish	$15.00	____
____	Trife Life To Lavish II	$15.00	____
____	Stackin' Paper II	$15.00	____
____	Rich or Famous	$15.00	____
____	Bitch A New Beginning	$15.00	____
____	Mafia Princess Part 1	$15.00	____
____	Mafia Princess Part 2	$15.00	____
____	Mafia Princess Part 3	$15.00	____
____	Mafia Princess Part 4	$15.00	____
____	Boss Bitch	$15.00	____
____	Baller Bitches Vol. 1	$15.00	____
____	Bad Bitch	$15.00	____
____	Princess Fever "Birthday Bash"	$9.99	____

Shipping/Handling (Via Priority Mail) $6.50 1-2 Books, $8.95 3-4 Books add $1.95 for ea. Additional book.

Total: $_____ **FORMS OF ACCEPTED PAYMENTS:** Certified or government issued checks and money Orders, all mail in orders take 5-7 Business days to be delivered.